Voices at the Quarry

D1568349

By

J. William Grimes

Contents

Dedication

To Spencer, lee, and Colby, my adult children.

Acknowledgments

Classmate Kent Carpenter, a college roommate whose career was a college professor, football coach and Dean of Men, provided me with much college campus detail and color.

William "Mickey McGowan, my brother in-law, whose career experience in the beer distribution business was invaluable in creating the set piece that gave the book a unique flavor.

About the Author

A native of West Virginia, Mr.Grimes graduated from West Virginia Wesleyan College with a degree in English. He moved to New York and had a successful career in media which included responsibility for CBS Radio's All-News Stations and president of cable network ESPN. For a decade he taught a graduate class, "Media Economics" in the evenings at the New School University.

The meeting of two
personalities is like the
contact of two chemical
substances: if there is any
reaction, both are
transformed.

— Carl Jung, Psychology and Religion

In the beginning, there was voice. When the only humans who existed were troglodytes cavemen, it was a voice, the sounding breath of life they discovered after climbing down from the trees. The voice made words and music that begat history. Sacred chants were born in immaculate churches in the former lands and ecclesiastical offshoots beyond. Human consciousness separated us from other animals, but it was the intelligible voice that fueled our ruling of all inhabitants of the land.

Chapter 1

"Show us your stuff, Scribe! Come back now; enough. Enough! You gotcha big balls, little man! Be careful, Scribe! Take the Dive. You can do it, Scribe."

The unforgiving sun, at its apotheosis, glared down upon the many. Crowd voices swelled in unison, and individual voices screamed out of tune.

Time stopped. The planet flattened. The year was 1960.

Student chants. *Go for it. Stop. Come down. Go for it. Stop. Come down. Jump. Stop. Take the Dive. You can do it, Scribe*

The drumbeat frenzy of the crowd voice.

The boy stood alone, his frail body wobbling in the wind at the edge of the boulder high above the soaring voices.

A comic book stick figure. He took a deep breath. The air was Appalachian springtime sweet. He'd removed his clothes except for his baggy Bermuda shorts and sneakers.

He looked skyward. For what? Redemption? Atonement? He looked below to see the faces of the voices, to hear their fierce song of goodbye.

He saw himself flying out into the starry universe, into the clutch of death or life anew. He'd decided the difference was minimal.

He gazed again at the voices below, irrelevant and ignorant. He removed a shoe and tossed it high into the world of others beyond the black water below. The voices screamed in splendid stereo as it fell like a dead duck into the maze of frolicking students.

He was of one with space and gravity, his place in the universe. The totality of his stay at the college, pictures of his parents on his dorm room desk, and friends Hal and the Dean. The articles he wrote for the college newspaper.

Every dream in his straight-A mind gyrated vividly in the circus of his mind.

He slithered to the edge of the boulder and glanced down at the cold black water of the rock quarry, which was reverberating with incoherent voices. He was where he belonged. Alone. Above it all.

"Go for it, Scribe. Take the dive, buddy. You're our hero. Show it, Scribe. the man." A chorus of students assembled on a grassy incline near the boulder and voiced in cheering unison, "S C R I B E. S C R I B E."

Chapter 2

Calvin College was a religious-affiliated, co-educational, liberal arts school located in the central part of the state. Built at the turn of the twentieth century with financial support from the United Council of Presbyterian Churches and with a handful of virgin timber and bituminous coal barons, the campus sat on the outskirts of Lewisburg, a town lodged comfortably between the gentle but commanding Appalachian foothills and the tapered hollows shouldering Birch River.

The campus occupied eighty acres of valley flatland, proudly exhibiting its eclectic architecture of Neoclassical, Georgian, Romanesque, and Southern Colonial buildings that fashioned a diverse aura which, it was claimed by the administration, helped attract twenty-five hundred students from fifteen states and a couple of nations.

In the first half of the Great American Century, Lewisburg was a bustling center of regional commercial activity. That had changed as vast new reserves of bituminous coal had been found hours away in the southern part of the state. Such discoveries negatively impacted coal prices from Lewisburg's mines, followed by the inevitable loss of jobs and population. At the same time, regional lumber companies were confronted with new competition from the pine forests of Georgia and the hardwood timberlands of northern Canada. Responding by guaranteeing finer quality products at lower prices, the lumber companies' profits plummeted, and the small firms shuttered. This economic misfortune plunged the entire region into economic torpor, and Lewisburg acquired the enervated look of a hoary athlete past his time.

In the decades of the Fifties and Sixties, Calvin students could be generally classified into four perceptible groups, each characterized by a dominant interest or activity. Representing maybe twenty percent of the student body were the pre-ministerial students, or "Pre-minnies," as they were called. Nearly all boys, were serious bible-studying scholars preparing academically for life as Presbyterian ministers. Their tuition payments were significantly discounted. The Church was still a major stakeholder, and it needed a continuing supply of new ambitious "Pre-minnies" to quell what looked like a slowdown in church attendance in the region. They formed their own close-knit society and were seldom seen beyond the campus.

The largest group, nearly equal in gender, represented about sixty percent of the student body and was modestly diverse in their academic interests— the boys usually majoring in business and accounting or phys ed and the girls in liberal arts and education. Often the first in their family to attend college, they participated in campus organizations and activities such as the student/faculty community council, college government, school newspaper, theater and chorale groups, and non-varsity secondary sports such as touch football and intramural basketball, baseball, soccer, tennis, and golf. Nearly half belonged to one of the seven Greek fraternities and sororities.

These students mingled effortlessly with the third group and fourth groups, which together represented the remaining fifth of the student body. They were the "Preps," active socializers, and the "Jocks," the varsity athletes of football and basketball. The Preps were modestly interested in education but were spectacularly active in social activities ranging from fraternity and sorority membership, spending hours at Calvin Student Center (CSC) and a portion of that at the Library, a large well-lit room, punching under their weight in time spent in the ivy suffused library building modeled upon New York City's Beaux-Arts library on Fifth Avenue. They were campus leaders in patronizing Lewisburg's two "road houses," located on the edge of town. Drinking alcohol anywhere, even off campus, in the Greek houses, or in the road houses, was grounds for dismissal though the administration didn't actively seek out the violators.

The Preps were snappily dressed, auto-enabled, and cash-carrying students. Most were from New York, New Jersey, and Connecticut and had begun their post-prep-school college life at more prestigious eastern schools. When they partied their way out of those institutions, no easy task, it was said a number of them every year found their way to Calvin College. This was good business for the college which was able to charge their parents the published tuition price, thus offsetting the school's financial deficit resulting from its generous support afforded the Pre-minnies and the Jocks.

The sixty or seventy Jocks, the varsity football and basketball players who were "full-boaters" whose tuition, room, and board were paid by the college and its donors.

Many Preps and Jocks belonged to the Theta Mu fraternity, which had the most members, the largest house, and the reputation as the rowdiest. The seemingly anomalous relationship between the Preps and the Jocks existed because the former, with more time on their hands and little interest in any academic endeavor requiring serious effort, were avid fans of the varsity teams. Far from city lights, many miles from a large university, and with only one available television channel, the football and basketball teams were major entertainment at Calvin. There would seldom be a game where the football stands and the basketball bleachers were not filled thirty minutes before game time with students, a handful of "townies, and professors, most of whom enjoyed live entertainment. The Jocks, mostly from modest-income homes, meshed well with the Preps because they were the major campus entertainers and most Preps found it cool to be seen in their company.

The Jocks produced thrills and stories on the home field and court. As reports of the teams' winning battles on enemy venues reached campus, the allure of the best-performing Jocks often became the news highlight of the day. These narratives of football and basketball success grew throughout the campus like kudzu vines, with the best players attaining star status among many students.

Such attraction, such student adulation, a desire to be "close" to Jocks, to get a response in kind when they said hello to —by name—of a Jock, particularly the star of the day or the week or season, was a moment of pleasure for many students. Not for the Preps, though; the Jocks knew most all their names and responded with star smiles when the Preps addressed them, or certainly when a Jock addressed a Prep who was valued because of his immediate ability to provide vehicular mobility, frequent complimentary beers at the roadhouses, and by association the companionship of the pretty girls who enjoyed the company and favors of the Preps.

It was said by a sociology professor that Calvin's student body mirrored that of Sixties' America: religiosity, industriousness, confidence, post-war frivolity, sports fandom, the freedom of exploration, and a willingness to try new things.

Chapter 3

It was a sun-suffused Saturday afternoon in late April at the rock quarry. Located within the two hundred-acre Mingo State Park about five miles from the campus, the rock quarry, or "The Quarry," as the Calvin students had affectionally lionized it with the capitalization because its location was perfect for springtime leisure. Surrounded by budding trees, flowering bushes, and early wildflowers, The Quarry was the preferred destination for student weekend lounging. A few decades ago, it was a bituminous coal mine until the mining company, realizing its supply of "black gold" was nearly depleted, decided it was advantageous to gift the property to the state. Lewisburg's mayor hailed this as a "substantial eleemosynary gesture by a private sector friend." Calvin's ministerial President echoed the sentiment, "The quarry will provide a venue for our students to relax from their extensive search for knowledge and to reflect upon God's gift of nature and life."

A subterranean river had been tapped to fill the quarry's crater, estimated one hundred feet deep. The water appeared jet-black which led to speculation that it was because the sun's rays were blocked half of every day by the towering boulder a few feet adjacent. Those inclined to doubt the story of the generosity of the mine's owner claimed it was coal mote seeping from below into the water that caused its ebony black color. Though often referred to as a "lake" for swimming, the water temperature in the warmest spring afternoon seldom reached sixty degrees, and as such, The Quarry's water was visited more by the eye than by the flesh.

Several tons of sand had been imported to create a twenty-foot-wide beach bordering the quarry, and scores of hybrid poplar and autumn maple trees had been planted along its two sides to retain the natural look of the surrounding locale. On sunny spring weekend days, the socially inclined would pile into cars with a plastic canister filled with ice and colas and a six-pack or two of Carling Black Label beer for those, mostly Preps, who feared not getting caught drinking at the Quarry. No student recalled ever seeing a college administrator at the Quarry. Here it should be noted that beer was the only viable alcoholic option for those violators of school policy. Liquor was only sold in state-owned stores and only to those twenty-one years of age and older. Student buyers'driver's licenses were carefully scrutinized except in the two roadhouses which did not sell liquor. The thinking was if a student got caught drinking beer at the Quarry or in a fraternity house or dorm, there would be some punishment, but if it were whisky, the student would be expelled with no second chance. And there was the spirit indigenous to the region, "Moonshine," a corn-distilled alcohol that was said to be available only from the "mountain men," an appellation ascribed to those overalled, often toothless, tobacco-chewing men who lived deep in the hollows, who produced in the hills and hollows. Moonshine was another thing occasionally touted by some Preps but never actually seen.

The Quarry was the preferred venue to snag some "downtime" after a modestly challenging academic week. The students indulged in sunbathing, card-playing, chilled drink consumption, and in the endless activity of talking incessantly about self, other students, parents, professors, movie stars, sports heroes, and occasionally politicians of note, usually the handsome young President of the United States and his elegant wife. The most popular subjects for the boys were which girls on campus they'd most like to lay; whether the nerdy president of the Glee Club was queer; which team, football or basketball, would have the higher winning percentage next season, and who was the funniest and most pathetic fraternity drunk.

The coeds garnered a substantial share of chit-chatting at The Quarry. Their popular issues were the reciprocity of their interest in the boy of the moment, the status of their back home high school crush, the style of their clothes, particularly their bathing suits, how terrible the dorm food was, and the personalities and emotional problems of girls not privy to their instant conversation. Runners-up in topicality, depending upon the composition of the girls, was which frat boy, or sometimes just any boy who most combined the older-brother brio of Pat Boone with the rough-and-tumble macho of John Wayne. Far and away and out of the boys' earshot, was how and when they would get their MRS degree. As improbable as it seems today that this would be an important issue, one needs to be reminded that in the 50s and 60s, only 15% of high school graduates went on to college, and most were boys. Post-war high-paying jobs in manufacturing were abundant throughout most of the nation, which negated the idea that further education was needed. For the coeds finding a husband in college was thought to be a much longer-term better prospect because the idea that a guy with a college degree was a much better long-term catch than the high school grad who worked in the steel mills or coal mines after high school Also the smart girls graduating from high school realized that would be more valuable, and fun, than staying in the hometown taking dictation from a bald VP at Citizen's Bank.

Chapter 4

When the spring sun's rays sizzled at The Quarry, many of the socially directed students reached for their bottles of mixed iodine and baby oil and partnered in applying it to every inch of visible skin. Ninety-eight percent of Calvin's students were white, and as incongruous as it may seem given the increasingly charged racial environment of the nation, it was cool to be as golden brown as possible. Maybe because it implied much leisure time and good health, or perhaps it was the recent popularity of Negro music that arrived at night from distant city AM radio stations. The girls could be heard rating the five best suntans other than their own while lounging on campus lawns where most of the tanning work would be done. The Quarry, visited mostly on weekends, would be the preferred place to deepen the tan and display it to the widest audience.

A spring weekend at the Quarry was seldom marked by curious minds consuming the content of great novels, philosophical treatises, or Gibbon's six-volume tome on the history of Rome. Textbooks or reading assignments were left in the dorm. The local weekly newspaper held little interest other than articles of Calvin's football and basketball teams' games and possibly the "Police Roundup section," a report that rarely cited a Calvin student misdemeanor, on rare occasions, a traffic violation. A Trustee of Calvin was the owner of the *Lewisburg Herald* and was astutely aware of the economic contribution the college made to the town, and anything negative about the school or the students was rarely seen in print. The girls brought magazines with movie stars on the covers, an occasional issue of *National Enquirer*, and books of crossword puzzles bundled in shoulder bags and sackcloth handbags. The boys sometimes brought an issue of *Sport* magazine or a copy of *Playboy* which, regardless of the issue date, would be wrinkled a day after a pass-around in the Theta Mu house. The transistor radio, a recent technological innovation, was an important media entertainment companion and a freshman coed from New Jersey gained instant popularity with her new Sony transistor model. Exciting stuff, even though only three radio stations could be received in the daytime hours and format selection was limited to religious programming on two, with the third featuring the "white music" of Pat Boone and Patti Page. On Sundays, the Sony was left at school; the three local stations served religious programming all day.

The Jocks mainly lounged in groups on the incline rising above the sand beach, where the best angles to steal a more revealing view of female chests were enhanced. Some brought a deck of cards and reveled in a competitive game of Hearts. Poker was more the Prep's pastime, but its preferred venue was in the fraternity houses. After a couple of beers, a few socially awkward boys would screw up their courage to mix with the girls. Few boys and zero girls braced the ominous black waters of The Quarry though many dipped a toe or hand mostly to attract the attention of those of the opposite sex who might be looking in their direction. The most exciting though seldom seen entertainment at The Quarry was "The Dive," the name given to a leap, a jump not a dive from a rocky ledge atop the prodigious boulder towering seventy feet above the icy water.

Achieving this feat required a demanding climb up a forty-five-degree angled stone slope to the plateau atop the boulder. There the boy, no girl ever attempted it, would have to take a ten-yard running start from the other end of the Boulder and accelerate rapidly so that his body would land in the deep water beyond the rocks on the shore below.

Of the students there that April day, only two had made The Dive: Bill Forrest, the star football running back, equally identified on campus for chain-smoking Pall Malls in the Calvin Student Center (CSC), and Joey Koppollo, a three-sport high school legend who in his two years at Calvin had yet to see action on field or court due to academic difficulties. Each attempted and executed The Dive only once. Everyone at The Quarry those two different days ceased whatever their amusement of the moment and watched, breath held, with unwavering astonishment as Forrest and Koppollo climbed the rock's ledge. After a moment of apparent indecision on the surface of the boulder, each sprinted and leaped feet-first, clearing the shore rocks by only a couple of yards and crashing into the black water. Pals stood at the water's edge with towels ready to warm the divers' bodies after a fifteen-yard gasping swim to a sandy shore.

Chapter 5

The seductive signs of spring were everywhere evident that day. The welcomed sunshine warmth of a cloudless sky interspersed with whispering wisps of crisp mountain air; the budding leaves of the maples in the early stage of summer green complementing the bold ashen and pink dogwood blossoms; and the hoary florets of the magnolia trees. There was the din of pristine spring: the chirping of the orange-breasted robins repairing their nests from the ill-tempered winter, the overhead cawing of emboldened crows annoyed perhaps by the arrival of students or hoping to snack on their edible inadvertent leavings, the tweeting pair of crimson cardinals streaking amidst the burgeoning foliage, and the buzzing zzzzzs of busy bees a flight in pre-season pollination. This operatic thrum teamed with the carefree chattering of boys and girls to produce an omnipresent orchestral song of springtime, an anthem of youthful mirth seldom heard on campus. The voices of privileged young people enjoying college life.

Here your writer must explain his use of the words "boys" and "girls" to label student genders at Calvin College. The conventional word for college males today is "men," but those who regularly habituated The Quarry back then weren't men – if its definition includes mature, highly responsible semi-adult young males.

17

"Boys" is the more accurate label based upon their often puerile, carefree, and self-centered conduct. The girls appeared more mature, wearing their practiced look of demure bearing though rumors of petty bickering over bathroom time in their dorm, table seating at meals, feuds over clothes, and the use of tears, heartfelt or not, employed as a weapon to settle disagreements were rumored in the frat houses. Noticeably in the presence of boys, the girls scored high in hiding their less attractive idiosyncrasies, jealousies, and other minor phobias. More girls than boys are learning to be but not quite yet, women and men.

An older student from Long Island who had served in the US Navy before enrolling at Calvin suggested the reason the students were "boys" and "girls' not men and women, was the womb-like isolation of the college's geographic location and the diminutive size of Lewisburg. "Seventy-five percent of these kids have never been to D.C, let alone Manhattan," he pronounced. And there was another reason. Neither gender had had the adult responsibilities of so many of those their age back in their home towns who were already in the full-time workforce, many married and on their way to parenthood. It was an idyllic, halcyon period in America. In such an environment, college kids perhaps mature later.

Chapter 6

Had T.S. Eliot been a Calvin College student visiting The Quarry on this April day, he would not have characterized it, even satirically, as the "cruelest month." For Jocks, there were no more grueling practices and bus travel to away football and basketball games. For the Preps, it was time to lower the roofs of their convertibles, slip on the madras shorts and don their shades. For all students, there was another reason to welcome this spring day. The "Cuban Missile Crisis" that brought the world near nuclear war, causing widespread student consternation, had been peacefully resolved.

A youthful resonance of frivolity resounded throughout The Quarry, tripping along the imported sand beach, rebounding off the imposing boulder, and skimming across the black water. It was a fine time to be a Calvin Cougar, the sports team's sobriquet, a reminder of the spotted coat, short tail cat species long ago kings of these hills now seldom seen.

Chapter 7

Hal Sparrow was a BMOC, a Big Man On Campus, admired by nearly all, even the Pre-minnies. Known as "Player," he sat cross-legged on an orange and black beach towel, Calvin's team colors. His chin rested Rodin Thinker style in the palm of his large hand, his eyes absorbing the expressions of a couple of dozen students standing and seated nearby on portable folding chairs and beach blankets, waiting to hear his opinion as to whether the Theta Mu fraternity should lose campus privileges after the hazing incident last weekend that resulted in the hospitalization of two pledges.

Player was a rare example of what college coaches and administrators frequently, and often disingenuously, called a "student-athlete." He had starred four years on the varsity basketball team, its captain the last two seasons, and majored in English, the only player on the team to do so. He had played a role in college productions of the Prince in "Hamlet" and Big Daddy Pollitt in "Cat on a Hot Tin Roof." He was a thoughtful, serious student who was seen more often in the school library than in the CSC, where most Jocks and Preps idled away the time between classes. The six-foot-four-inch backcourt man, an ever contender for Dean's List, earned his academic achievements not by the innate intellect but by a highly disciplined work ethic burnished at a military academy where he prepped. While one of the most recognized students on campus, on a sociability scale with metrics such as close friendships, party-going, and fun-loving, he would rank below the middle of the pack. Very few students knew Hal Sparrow. He shunned the courtship of the fraternities, remaining an "independent." While congenial with those whose company he chose to share, he was reserved and private. His steady girl friend, Janet Ingram, had graduated a year earlier and was teaching elementary school in Pittsburgh. They planned to marry after his graduation though no date had yet been set.

Besides Janet, only Hal Sparrow's roommate in his first year, Norman Emory, knew the personal details of Player's life. Hal was brought up in a home of parental distress until high school, when he was invited to attend and board a private military academy outside Pittsburgh. His two older sisters had left home by the time he was eight years old, and his mother supported the family as a substitute school teacher. His father's lack of interest in continuous occupation became more evident, and he struggled to find work. When she was teaching and his father was home, he would rebuke Hal over trifling faults for minor omissions and behavior the father disliked. The castigations became increasingly more severe. As children learn from the behavior of their parents, Hal learned from these unhappy experiences that it was not in his interest to defend himself from these verbal assaults, particularly when his father had been drinking, which was frequent. His mother's increasing anger at his father's selfish misbehavior led to more quarreling and to parental confrontations, which invariably had negative consequences for Hal. His father's physical and emotional distance from his mother, coupled with intimating threats and reprisals hurled by each to the other, prompted Hal to retreat into passive acceptance, a "peace at any price" syndrome often a characteristic of intimated, abused youths. He learned avoiding confrontation was in his best interest. The refuge was gained by obedient compliance and the absence of self-expression.

And it was this domestic environment that stimulated Hal's interest in sports, basketball in particular. On outdoor courts in the summer, in school gymnasiums, and at the YMCA in winter, the boy found solace from the growing chaos at home. He spent endless hours shooting baskets and playing pickup games. Because it was a game that also could be played alone, basketball was the perfect antidote for the cacophony and discord that existed at home. His failure to confront his father and his fear that either parent might resort to violence, or leave him, inhibited the expression of his emotions and suppressed the maturation of his ego. As a result, Hal found his source of recognition, achievement, and freedom in sports, where his athletic ability and modesty gained the respect of his fellow athletes, mostly older boys. Parental in the way older boys sometime mentor younger players with talent; they lifted his spirits and became his proxy family. Hal never missed an opportunity to play the game with or without others. Daily, his status as a gifted and competitive player grew, and it would be only a slight overstatement to say he became known in the city of Pittsburgh as a playground luminary by eighth grade.

Chapter 8

On this day at The Quarry, students were engaged in discussions of the biggest story on campus since the basketball team lost in overtime in the conference tournament finals, the fraternity hazing, and what degree of punishment the school should mete out to Theta Mu for allegedly forcing two members of their spring pledge class to drink some kind of whiskey leading to their hospitalization. A forthcoming decision to be made by a committee consisting of representatives from the administration, faculty, and student body had been expected Thursday. It was now Saturday, and no word yet. Everyone had an opinion as to what the punishment should be depending upon his or her own personal experiences, biases, and hopes.

Player was one of two student members on the disciplinary committee as he listened to the heated discussion. There was a pause as cans of beer were passed around. Then Player spoke.

"The college has clear and well-circulated rules regarding alcohol usage. There is no argument on that, right?" He paused, heads nodding in synch. "And the Greek Society and the college have agreed-upon rules regarding hazing, defining it and spelling out what kind of hazing activities fraternity brothers can compel pledges to undertake. In other words, what kinds of pre-membership hazings are acceptable? And the fraternity leaders know all this, right?"

Player looked around the beach vista, observing the usual student groupings and activities. There were the Theta Mu preps seated on folding chairs with the winsome Delta sorority girls and the southern gentlemen Kappa Chi's, the boys who donned Confederate uniforms on Homecoming Weekend now more or less engaged in spirited chat with girls from what was known as the "literary' sorority, the Alpha Gams. There were a few football guys looking a little larger in their swimsuits after months off the field, arm wrestling, and playing Hearts. Others, not so easily identified by the homogeneity of group association, were engaging in mutually applying sun tanning lotion, digging skillfully into the styrofoam chests selecting the beverage of choice, and skimming the pages of popular magazines while simultaneously talking to three or more companions, and listening to two others.

Each student in Player's audience simultaneously nodded their assent to his hypothesis on the issue at hand except one, Kent Ayers, the Theta Mu president who had been dealing with the problem all week. His look of disinterest and mild annoyance indicated he wanted to put this discussion out of his mind, or at least out of earshot. Why he was even standing here listening to Hal

Sparrow "Player" shape the issue, he didn't know. And, as if to rectify his apparent disinterest in Player's role in the matter, Ayers looked across the vista to the rock quarry where a caravan of student cars was arriving, competing for parking spaces. Soon the voices of those in favor of severe punishment for his fraternity would increase, babbling like the nearby brook that fed into the Birch River after the snow melted.

Player listened with evident attentiveness to opinions expressed on the conduct of Theta Mu seniors like Ayers, who had responsibility for the fraternity's indoctrination of new members. The same physical gestures and facial expressions which characterized his on-court mien, the aggressive pose of his jutting jaw, the coordinated movement of his hands, and the sparkling intensity of his gray eyes were clearly visible. As he sat in full concentration mode, leaning in towards his gathered followers, a bulky white cloud appeared from nowhere and passed overhead, diminishing the sun's brilliance, casting a momentary pall on Player's face, underscoring the gravity of the discussion and his role in the issue.

"And all the fraternities know they are not permitted to serve alcohol to pledges under any circumstances. Let's not forget the use of alcohol is prohibited by the College." A few in the audience smirked. "But we know that rule is occasionally honored more in the breach than in the observance," he said with a slight nod to acknowledge the faint smile of one or two who recognized this line from "Hamlet," a line he had spoken in his starring role.

Kent Ayers twisted his face in guarded acceptance as Player continued.

"The brother in charge of pledging would be the one directly responsible, correct? Where was he?" Player directed this query, not at Ayers, because that might indicate a bias against the fraternity, and as a committee member whose role was to adjudicate the matter, he did not want to show any bias. Instead, he turned his gaze to Bo Dotson, a member of Kappa Sigma and the Inter-Fraternity Council, an elected group of one representative from each of the school's seven Greek chapters. Ayers looked on in apparent relief.

Dotson was on his feet. This was his matter, too; he had skin in this game. "This is a big screw-up, no doubt, Player. One of the gigantic proportions. But can any of us say with assurance that there was no general member oversight? More likely, could it have been one non-thinking member who neglected his responsibility; causing this? Where's the evidence there was any institutional wrongdoing? I haven't heard any." He glanced at Ayers, who seemed lost in thought, wondering why the hell he had come to The Quarry today.

Dotson continued, "I don't know where the blame should be placed, but twenty pledges were there that night, and only two got sick. That indicates to me that pledges were not forced to drink that moonshine or whatever it was they allegedly drank." He paused to light up a smoke. A sudden breeze whirled down from the boulder behind the quarry, and Bo had to flick the spark wheel of his cigarette lighter two more times to get that cool menthol taste of the King-sized Kool.

"This hazing stuff has been going on for years," he continued, voice rising. "It's all part of the fraternity brotherhood process. I know you never were into that Player, but this is the first time we seniors have experienced any irregularities with hazing. I'd say our Greek behavior during our four years here has been on the square."

Player searched the faces for agreement or not. No one spoke.

Kent Ayers, emboldened perhaps by Dotson's support, turned to the crowd. "Thanks, Bo. It's our fraternity, my fraternity. And each member is immensely proud of our contribution to campus activities and life here at Calvin. We work hard to be responsible student citizens, and I might add responsible members of the

Lewisburg community. Every year we organize a Beautify Lewisburg Day, which, as you know, we brothers work with the local business owners to clean the streets, paint walls of designated buildings and make our college town more beautiful." He inhaled a puff of the mountain spring air and paused to signal the import of what he would say next.

"Something happened out there that night. We don't know yet exactly what it was, but we soon will believe me. And, Bo, no one has said it was moonshine the guys drank. Let's stick to what we know." Heads nodded in meager approval. Every Theta Mu president in Player's time at Calvin possessed the verbal skill of a lawyer to advocate for the interests of his fraternity. Ayers looked around the group seeking agreement.

Bethany Pearson, the reigning Homecoming Queen, with her unhurried intonation honed at a girl's preparatory school in South Carolina, was perched on a director's chair in a one-piece green swimming suit that accentuated her fluttering emerald eyes. She brushed back a snippet of flaxen hair, a distinct mannerism she frequently exhibited at the CSC gatherings to solicit even greater attention from those who found her alluring looks irresistible.

"Let's remember," she began, "these kids were freshmen who've never been away from home. I don't

29

know either one, but I heard they were kind of strange guys, not Theta types." A couple of heads nodded in agreement. Bethany continued. "They probably never had much to drink, like maybe never. Boys get here away from Mommy and Daddy and get carried away with the freedom of being out of the nest. Look, Player," she said with a beaming solemn gaze, "maybe they were drinking before the pledge stuff started. Who knows? But, I would ask Kent who were these pledges' big brothers and where were they that night? It's a black eye for all Greeks, but as Bo said, only two of twenty got sick, and I don't think you can be too harsh on the fraternity. Freshmen have to take some responsibility for their actions."

Bonnie Edwards, normally a taciturn girl of modest allure who seemed ever pleased to be in Bethany's reflected glow, purred: "Exactly. Exactly".

Player focused on the two coeds. "In sororities, there is no hazing. Right?"

"Well, not that kind…." Bethany's voice drifted off with the breeze, merging into the myriad of background jabber before being consumed by the hovering hills and hungry hollows.

Bonnie sat up on her blanket and peaked to say something. "You know, Bethy, you might think differently if those boys were your brothers or your sons.

Just sayin'." Heads nodded again. Bonnie said again. "Just sayin'."

The sound of the Chiffons singing "He's So Fine" interrupted the momentary silence. The girl from New Jersey with the Sony had arrived.

Chapter 9

Norman Emory had arrived, edging his way into the circle and settled on a blanket next to a couple who were seldom separated from each other on or off campus. During his freshman year, when he roomed with Hal Sparrow, Norman, as editor of the monthly college newspaper, *The Pharos*, and a frequent contributor to the weekly *Lewisburg Gazette*, became known as "Scribe." During his four years at Calvin ,the ubiquity, topicality, and incisiveness of his journalistic and opinion pieces attracted a larger audience; Scribe garnered widespread campus recognition and was increasingly a sort of revered celebrity. He was thought to be an intellectual and did nothing to upend that student mindset. He, too, in a very different way from Player was a BMOC. His popularity was enhanced by his peripatetic personality. He seemed to be everywhere at once, prompting humorous speculation there was more than one Scribe Emory on campus. Doubles. Though solicited for brotherhood by two fraternities, Scribe, like Player, remained independent. He was one of those very few students on campus who appealed to every group: Pre-minnies liked him because he saw to it that news of their religious activities was given front-page exposure in *The Pharos*. Many knew him from their classes or by working with him on one of his numerous campus leadership organizations and found him generous with his time and highly focused on group goals. The Jocks liked him because no one on campus was a bigger fan of the football and basketball teams. He was invariably among the first to arrive for a game at the stadium and field house and the last to leave. He often would holler out encouragement when the players needed it or shriek in fury when an official blew a call. He knew every meaningful team and individual statistic, reciting each with enthusiasm to eager audiences at the CSC. He wrote every story of Calvin's football and basketball games for both newspapers. When the Cougars won, he exuberantly praised the play of the standout performers; when they lost, his articles offered a frank appraisal of individual lapses: naming who dropped passes or missed layups. Never unfair or overly harsh, the players respected his opinions and loved talking sports with him. The Preps, too, found Scribe a jitterbug of kinetic energy talking to one and all and taking notes on the small pad he carried in his pants back pocket. He mentioned he was taking notes to finish a novel, and word spread campus-wide like a weather forecast for a sunny spring Saturday. One prep, John P. Forbes III, known as Three Stick Johnny, exalted for his ownership of a classic mustard yellow Edsel convertible and envied for his two-bedroom party apartment off campus was so enamored with Scribe's journalistic stature that one spring break, he invited him to his home in New Jersey to meet his father who owned a string of local weekly newspapers. Scribe politely declined an offer of employment after graduation wanting to remain near home and begin a career as a journalist at the *Pittsburgh Gazette.*

Scribe seemed to have no female interest, at least not with any particular girl though he was liked by all the prettiest, most popular, and smartest coeds. At the CSC, he would often be seen in a booth with two or three vivacious coeds cheerfully engaged in conversation about campus happenings, their activities, and relationships. Some speculated that he was queer based upon his falsetto voice and that he was never seen with one girl though there was not a shred of evidence to support this gossip..

*   *   *

Scribe appeared that day at The Quarry, wearing shabby khakis, a gray T-shirt with faded orange letters CALVIN, Keds sneakers, and a baseball cap with the letter P for Pirates on its crown. He was maybe five-foot-six and weighed no more than one hundred and twenty pounds. His wide-rim eyeglasses seemed to make his undersized face appear even smaller while accentuating its wan chalky hue. His jet-black hair was thinning, which made him look older and more professorial. Later those present would disagree with what his facial expression signaled that day. Some said he looked detached, indifferent. Others said drowsily. Norman was never known for his ebullience or as a "fun guy," but today, there was a hitch in his walk, a different intonation in his voice, and his unworldly bearing.

Player was surprised to see him based upon what he had heard in their morning breakfast meeting. A mild ripple emerged among those nearby sensing he would have something significant to say on the issue at hand. But only Player knew the troubles that occupied the boy's mind.

Not known as a drinker, Scribe moved to a position on an incline guaranteeing that all in the crowd would clearly see him. Offered a can of beer, he took a gulping swallow and cleared his voice. All eyes pivoted to him as his own rotated between Bo Jenkins and Kent Ayers.

"Hail, brothers and sisters, citizens of Calvin and the world," he began stolidly. "This is not a banner time at Calvin. I know everyone is consumed with this hazing issue. I'd like to make a brief comment or two about it."

For an instant, while the crowd chatter diminished, he looked skyward as if his rhetoric were housed somewhere above the clouds.

"Maybe the Theta brothers got carried away with what they thought was acceptable hazing. Or, maybe the pledges got carried with all that moonshine, or beer, or whatever it was, but let's not forget freshmen boys often don't know what's really happening, don't fully understand the literal world they find themselves in, and said more prosaically they don't know their ass from their elbows. And fraternity members have an obligation to be good brothers, to provide guidance when necessary, and not conduct themselves like KKK's in white sheets on lonely back roads where something bad happened that night. The whole idea of hazing, when you think about it, is a dark anachronism, tribal voodoo, a wicked hangover from the Dark Ages. Think about it. Hazing should be discontinued. Fraternity leaders should sit down and agree to end it once and for all. Think of its effect upon our school, to be one of the first colleges in the nation where the fraternities agreed, not remanded, to end hazing forever." He spread long arms wide and abundantly, a benevolent leader, Jesus-like. "Show leadership and ban this sadistic ritual."

There were voices of mild agreement as he paused and accepted a can of Fort Pitt, took a short chug, and returned it to its owner.

"Come on, Scribe, some slack." It was Bo Dotson, Kappa Sig again. "Shit happens, and we're all sorry about it. The pledges survived. OK? The committee Player's on will decide what penalty if any, will be handed down, and none of us innocents here will be affected either way except maybe Kent," he said, looking over at the silent Theta Mu chief with a "we're-all-good-fellows" pseudo smile. "I never liked the Theta's anyway, present company excepted."

A chorus of chuckles. Bo was a Prep who spoke first and thought next, a witty guy in his own mind.

Geno Remley, a day student popular for hosting parties in his parents' playroom basement, spoke. "We're here to have some fun; enjoy the day, Scribe. Loosen up. Good work, wise words, Scribe. I've got another brew for you when you finish that one." Voices chirped with relief of a break from the heaviness surrounding the hazing discourse. Those near Scribe chuckled nervously as he drained the last few ounces from the can and, hitching up his pants that appeared to be struggling to maintain their position on his waist, he continued, without indicating in any way he would accept the advice to loosen up. Unless you were to believe his consuming, a couple of ounces of beer was loosening up.

"The brothers want, shall we say demand, that pledges adhere to the traditions of their fraternity. The word brother is used to strengthen the appeal of membership, suggesting by obvious implication that all members support each other in times of doubt, in times of need, and in times of fraternal affiliation. A pledge is recruited, sought out by the members, and promised to share the fraternity's particular union of fellowship to be a chosen brother. Fraternity is a word derived from the Latin *fraternitatem,* which means the sharing of common interests. The pledge is obviously in search of being in common with the members with whom he obviously feels happy and important to become a member with them. More importantly, can a fraternity pledge in any way benefit from being hazed? Hard to believe he could anyway like it, enjoy it."

Scribe stopped. The crowd of listeners had grown, two or three feet deep in a semi-circle with eyes upon him. His head gravitated left to right and then back again as if seeking a frown of disagreement or a grim expression of acceptance.

"The question is whether fraternity members provided and or encouraged the boys to consume the alcoholic drink. We don't know that yet, and I won't speculate and suggest you do not either. But what we do know is a small group of faculty and students, including Player here, will meet early next week to sort this out, provide a statement of their findings and recommend a future course of action, if required. And let's be thankful that, I'm told; both boys were in classes yesterday."

A few voices rose in agreement. Hands shot up.

Scribe waved them off.

"Hold on. The values and traditions of fraternities and sororities are not wrong. To join a group and affiliate with like-minded others is a human pattern, an evolutionary instinct. But what does hazing have to do with it? How does hazing help the pledge's understanding of the traditions, the values of the fraternity?"

He paused as if to implore a response that did not come.

"As we have just seen, hazing can put a pledge's health at risk. Is hazing, meaning some physical and potentially dangerous activity imposed upon others who cannot respond, a necessary requirement of those accepted to join the brotherhood to be subordinated for a time to prove their loyalty to their member brothers to be? Is it brotherly love? Sounds a bit like what the Mafia requires a young mob subordinate to become a made man, I think they call it, by making him take a knife and cut a slice of a finger to produce draw blood; yes, I know this is not a rational analogy but please forgive me, I am becoming overly emotional. Two young boys out of town late at night in the company of their brothers drinking alcohol in the middle of the night? Then at some time hospitalized. It hurts."

As Player rose from the beach towel he had been

sitting upon as if to signal to Scribe that it was time to relinquish the podium, a thin bespeckled student of average height appeared, walking through the assembled students towards the boys. Heads turned to see Tom Bolyard, a senior and president of the Pre-Ministerial Fellowship; an organization opened to all students though the majority were Presbyterian boys, known by those interested by its motto "To all the world, the gospel." Voices were quieted as Bolyard reached Scribe, who had also ceased his discourse.

"Scribe, please excuse me. Just for a moment. I, we, have heard your views on what happened that night, and I think all here share your feelings, your hurt." Scribe sent a nodding glance and took a couple of steps back. All eyes were now focused on Bolyard, who few knew, and many did not recognize. Pre-minnies were seldom seen at the Quarry. Player thought the only reason Bolyard was making his rare visit today was to comment on the incident that was top of mind for most.

Unlike most students at the Quarry that warm day with a bright sun who were wearing khakis and Bermuda shorts the minister to-be wore a long sleeve gray shirt and gray cotton trousers with cuffs an inch or two above the top-line of his shoes. He had fully extended his arms, horizontal to his waist, with the inside of his hands showing, his fingers separated as though in preparation to catch a large ball, the gesture comprehensively similar to various depictions of Jesus welcoming his followers. "Thank you, Norman," choosing instead the seldom used, likely unknown by many, Scribe's first name.

"Brothers ands sisters, we are here together at this Christian college, this citadel of learning, by the grace and love of God. He took his son so that our sins were absolved. We are born sick and ignorant, and it's with God's love and blessing that we are given another chance to love him and Jesus and each other. About these two young men who were hospitalized. They were what the fraternities call pledges meaning these two Christians were committed to become brothers of an on-campus fraternity. But they and we are all brothers and sisters during our brief stay at Calvin. It is God's will that we all must strive to love each other, and to treat each other kindly. Life without friendship and empathy is only selfish existence. And hazing is inhuman. I say it, and I say it again, hazing must be stopped." If there is something like a silent applause, it was at tis moment. Students nodded, and the moment of silence was interrupted only by birds' songs and tweets and the thrum of the nearby brook.

Player snapped the solemnity of the moment. "Tom, thank you for your wise words. Let's all enjoy this beautiful day and be thankful for what we have here at

Calvin." With that, he breathed deeply and looked at Scribe, and frowned. If Scribe wanted another beer, he would discourage it. But the boy walked away with a can in hand, and Player remained silent.

Chapter 10

Hal Sparrow and Norman Emory met four years ago on their first day at Calvin. Hal arrived by bus from Pittsburgh with one large suitcase stuffed with all the clothes he had. Situated between shirts and pants in his sport coat pocket was two hundred dollars in cash he had saved from his summer job at the beer warehouse and his prep school yearbook signed by pals from Pittsburgh and Cleveland he thought he'd never see again. He knew not one would be coming to Calvin, and after college, they'd go to graduate school or to New York to begin a career in banking. Some would return to work in their father's business or take a management training position at US Steel or the H.J. Heinz corporation, both headquartered in Pittsburgh. A few of his teammates at Sewickly Prep, who like him, were on scholarship for their football and basketball prowess, would return to their homes in the city's smoky neighborhoods and the coal mining and hardscrabble farm towns nearby. The tri-state region, consisting of western Pennsylvania, eastern Ohio, and northern West Virginia, was experiencing an economic downturn. Several steel plants had closed, resulting from foreign competition, and job opportunities for a young men, particularly those without a college education and social connections, were diminishing. That was the main reason Hal had studied hard and scored good grades, which, along with his success in two sports at Sewickly produced the opportunity to attend Calvin College on a full scholarship. He wanted to avoid a life in the mills and never see his Duquesne neighborhood again.

He stepped off the bus early that afternoon in Clarkston, a small city twenty miles north of Calvin College. From there, he hitched a ride to Lewisburg. It so happened the car that stopped and offered him a lift was occupied by a man, his wife, and his son, who was also enrolling at Calvin as a freshman. Hal sat in the back seat next to the quiet boy whose name was Turner and listened attentively as the mother described what a perfect college Calvin was.

"A beautiful, tree-lined campus with nice, clean-cut kids, like Turner," and after a perceptible pause and a turn of her head to face the boys in the backseat said, "Calvin has such a safe environment," which Hal thought meant no Negros or kids with three-syllable last names, those from tough neighborhoods like his, adding, "And best of all," she intoned with authority, "it's a Protestant school with small classes and professors who really care about their students. I, we know that because we've visited several quality colleges," glancing at them with what Hal thought was a practiced smile and then as if in a moment of self-introspection, she shared her benevolence with her taciturn husband behind the wheel.

With a slight swivel of his head he said in a subordinated tone, "That's true, mom." With that vocal solaced support, or likely even had he said nothing, she continued with a lift in her voice. "And no college has a better student-to-professor ratio. Or is it the opposite, professor-to-school ratio, silly me. Oh, what the heck, it doesn't really matter, does it, Turner." It was not a question.

But she had one. "And you, son. What's your name again?"

Before Hal could answer, she remembered. "Oh yes, Bird. No, no, my fault. It's Sparrow." She seemed untroubled by her inconsequential faux pas. Because it was hers.

"And you, Mr. Sparrow, do you agree with me about these unique advantages of Calvin?" It was a question designed to elicit a compatible response. How could he here, a passenger with no ticket, disagree?

"Yes, ma'am, that's what I heard. Haven't seen the campus yet."

Which produced a whispering "woo" from the passenger front seat followed by stillness for maybe a quarter of a mile.

Turner broke through the silence in an admiringly faint voice, "Are you, is it Hal, a ballplayer?"

Looking down upon the small boy Hal said, "I guess

45

you could say that. I'm here to get an education, but the coach says I can play basketball here."

The invisible father behind the wheel came to life, his head rotating forty-five degrees to take a good look at Hal.

"Good stuff, Mr. Sparrow. I am, we are, big fans of Calvin sports. Well, I should say after Penn State, of course. We live near Happy Valley, but I know the Cougars are always near the top of their conference in sports."

"And education, Warren," the mother reminded the father, who Hal thought didn't need the reminder.

"That's good, sir, and hope we stay there," said Hal responding to Warren, who seemed coming to life.

The mother was back. "Yes. We like Penn State for football, but Turner," as if the boy wasn't there, "needs a small school, a family environment. And Calvin is perfect. He's the kind of boy who will fit in fine here. Penn State is the United Nations. No offense but not for Turner."

Hal thought there were advantages to not having a mother.

Ahead he saw the sign: Lewisburg 5M.

The mother turned in her seat, a three-quarter face fixed on Hal. "It's none of my business, son, but where are your parents, if I may ask?"

Having already asked, Hal had no choice but to answer. "Well, my mom's passed away, and my dad, I don't see too much. I am pretty independent, spent my last four years at a boarding school near Pittsburgh."

The woman didn't comment, wasn't interested in his biography, probably feeling superior that Turner had Warren, a father who was not too busy to accompany him to his first day of college, and of course, a living, loving mother who was there for her son. A boy with no mother, she couldn't imagine. She'd never let that happen to Turner.

Hal wondered how Turner felt about his mother's pontifical attitude. He imagined the boy more a fan of his father. Hal thought it would be nice having a father he liked.

On the street overlooking the school's campus and buildings, Hal jumped out of the car, thanked them, and said to Turner, "Let's catch up sometime." While the family drove off to find a place to park, Hal crossed the lawn of the campus in the direction of several buildings. Students were everywhere, ambling and scrambling, following or leading their parents mostly to one building which Hal concluded must be where incoming freshmen registered. He found the gothic three-story stone structure to be the Administration Building and walked through the open door joining a line of chatting kids filling out requisite forms with the oversight of anxious parents. He was soon attended to by a prim-looking woman seated behind a desk with a maze of folders alphabctically arranged. "Hello, mam, my name is Sparrow. Hal Sparrow. I'm a freshman looking to register. Am I in the right place?"

"Yes indeed, Hal Sparrow, we're expecting you. Welcome to Calvin College. I see you will be living in Blake Hall, our newest dormitory. I think you will be quite comfortable there. Here's your packet of information. All you'll need to know to get started."

He found a bench on the lawn under a sprawling oak tree and opened the legal-sized envelope. Included was a list of his scheduled classes with building and room number and professors' names and a campus map with his dormitory, Blake Hall, identified in red letters, and two-room keys as well as a schedule for times meals were served in the student dining room. Also, there was a handwritten note from Coach Allen Andrews requesting his presence tomorrow in the gymnasium at 4 PM to meet with him and other incoming basketball prospects.

Hal walked the steps to the second floor of Blake Hall to room number 211. The door was half open, and standing inside; he saw the back of a frail boy who was in the process of hanging on the wall above one of the two beds a poster picture of Roberto Clemente, the Pittsburgh Pirates all-star outfielder next to one of Bobby Lane, the Steelers quarterback. The room was about 12 by 20 feet, housing two single beds situated against the opposite walls, two small desks with chairs, clothes closets at the wall near the foot of each bed, and one thin curtained window situated between the desks overlooking the campus lawn.

The boy turned around and looked at Hal, a smile arriving on his sunless face dominated by eyeglasses that magnified the size of his eyes. He was wearing a blue sweatshirt with gold letters reading PIRATES. Maybe this Pittsburgh sports fan, his roommate assuming he was in the right room, was a ballplayer, but if so, it sure wouldn't be football or basketball. Maybe there was a horse racing team, and he was a jockey, Hal chuckled to himself; all this passed through his mind in less than the time than it took to release his jump shot.

Sitting on one bed was a serious-looking man studying a sheaf of papers like the ones Hal was holding. A woman was placing folded clothes in neat piles in the chest of drawers. The boy spoke in a high-pitched voice, "You must be Hal, Hal Sparrow, my roommate!"

"And you are Norman Emory if I am in the right room."

"Yes, I am," the boy replied, stepping towards Hal. "I've never had a roommate before other than my sister, and that was for only a little while." He sent a wide smile personalized, thought Hal for himself. A friendly little fellow. With a returned smile, Hal offered his hand, and Norman Emory grasped it with a hard hold, shaking it with an eagerness Hal had experienced only with his basketball coach after a win featured by a late-quarter comeback. Hal placed his suitcase on the other bed, unmade with a set of sheets, two blankets, and a pillow. It appeared to be about his length, seventy-six inches, and maybe twenty-some in width.

"So, Hal, I'm new at being a roomie. I hope you will overlook any initial miscues or turnovers; I should say, so please let me know if I do anything annoying. I'm a pretty quick learner; try not to make the same mistake twice."

The man and woman were now on their feet with welcoming smiles of their own. Norman introduced his parents. Hal bowed ever so slightly; not one of the three exceeded five-nine. He also wondered if they, too, like Turner's mother thought it odd, he was here alone.

Hal began to unpack. Norman spoke. "I know you are from Pittsburgh. Me, too. Actually, from McKeesport. And you're from Duquesne, in the city, right?"

Hal replied, "Yep, near where the two rivers become

one, close enough to the mills to see the big smokestacks and occasionally the sun."

Norman chuckled as he placed a framed photograph on his desk. Thinking it was another photo of a Pittsburgh sports illuminary, Hal paused an instant to get a better look. What he saw in the frame was a head-to-chest photograph of presumably his new roommate's parents and a young girl. His father wore a navy blue military jacket adorned with golden epaulets, a handful of medals, and a peaked hat with a visor and cap badge. His mother was smiling radiantly in a green dress with a matching ribbon in her auburn hair. And the young girl with long braided brown hair and eyeglasses wore the harmed expression of preferring to be somewhere else. Hal felt a twinge of envy. He had no photos of his family, what was left of it, but he was pleased for his new roommate, who obviously was so happy with his family that he wanted to be reminded of them every day.

With the family picture now set at the perfect angle towards Norman's pillow, the boy focused again on Hal. "I know you played football and basketball at Sewickly, the private school north of the city. I remember reading about your hoops playoff games this past March. Great to meet you, roomie."

Hal looked at him, more than a little surprised. "How could you know that?"

"I was editor of my high school newspaper and wrote the sports stories. I kept up with most of the conferences throughout the area. And, here at Calvin, I have already applied for a reporting spot on The Pharos, the school paper."

Hal glanced at Norman's parents, who were nodding with pride. His father said, "Norman is being a little modest. He's not always that way, so you're forewarned." They all laughed, a little nervously. "It was his journalistic abilities that earned him some financial aid here."

Norman, reacting as if pricked by a pin, said, "Come on, dad. That's not neat." And then, "Wouldn't it be great, Hal, if someday I could write about you? 'Hal Sparrow leads Cougars to the conference championship victory.' I brought my typewriter with me. It will be on the desk, and you can use it if you ever need to write your papers." After saying their goodbyes, Norman told Hal he planned to major in English. Hal was excited and pleased. That was his plan too. Taking classes with a roommate, studying together, and being able to conveniently discuss their assignments should be a big plus. Lying in his bed that night, he felt fortunate with what he had in common with this small, bookish boy, and what he didn't would make being roommates even more interesting.

Chapter 11

Hal Sparrow, at six-four, weighed a rock solid one-eighty. He had a full head of hazel brown hair and gray eyes with twenty-twenty vision. Norman, on tiptoes, was maybe five foot seven and not a pound over one-thirty. His head, disproportionately large for his frame, was dominated by his charcoal hair and thick black-framed eyeglasses. Hal thought Norman looked the way an English major and newspaper reporter should, attentive, verbal, and energetic. Hal's decision to major in English was heavily influenced by his academic advisor at Sewicley and his difficulty incomprehending relative to his classmates any science or math-related course after Plane Geometry which he passed with an influencing assist from his two coaches.

He and Norman soon met other freshman boys who lived in the dorm. Because they were together so often those first couple of weeks –-they usually dined together, took two classes together, and often went to the library after dinner—they became known to those on their floor as Mutt and Jeff, a reference to the newspaper comic strip duo about the adventures of Jeff, a big athletic kid, and Mutt his small pal who were always together.

Spending so much time together in Room 211 with the shared choice of study and interest in sports fostered the rapid development of their friendship. Often before retiring for the evening, conversations began with an exchange of high school memories of good friends, idiosyncratic teachers, star athletes, summer jobs, and other leisure time activities. There were stories one told that resonated with the other because of a related or similar experience the other had. Part of that was the geographic location, part mutuality of interests, and part serendipitous. Sometimes these shared memories produced spontaneous laughter. Hal told about the time in eighth grade when his basketball team, with a first-year coach, traveled an hour to the opponent's gym for a big game only to discover upon arrival they were at the wrong school in the wrong county. Norman told of an oral report he was to make on the comedic differences between Shakespeare and Ben Johnson's plays. When called to stand and deliver, he discovered he did not have his notes and had left them at home. Hal laughed. "Like the dog eating your homework." While discussing how the Steelers played so much better at home last season, they realized they both had been spectators at the Pittsburgh Class AAA high school football championship game last November played at Forbes Field, the home of Pirates and Steelers. Hal was there with his basketball coach and teammates; Norman was present as a member of a group of a dozen select area high school newspaper editors charged with writing a two-thousand-word article about the game. The papers would be judged by editors of the *Pittsburgh Gazette*, with the three best awarded a cash prize. He confessed to a third-place finish. Hal thought that was great. They relished with the fact they were both winners in their own domains: basketball player and journalistic writer, but as they became more comfortable with each other, they also acknowledged had each been a little better at their pursuits, Hal would have been suiting up at Pitt or Penn State and Norman writing at Swarthmore or Penn. From candor, empathy, and admission of a small disappointment or two, a deeper personal connection was forged.

Chapter 12

Autumn arrived late that last year of the Fifties, resplendent in its display of red and yellow hues of the deciduous trees that dominated the campus grounds. The sun's spectacular September luster accompanied the students' new experiences, thoughts, opinions, and self-doubt. On Columbus Day, a sudden rain shower arrived with the unwelcome reminder that summer was over. The crispness in the air seemed to accompany the students' inclination to interact more confidently with each other, or at least with those living in closer proximity. Roommates' discussions of high school experiences, friends back home, and new people they were meeting had begun to give way to more meaningful, more personal discussions. Norman and Hal shared anecdotes about family, initiated by Norman being more open to expressing his feelings. Hal's reserve, his introspection, and his concealed unhappy parental memories would prove more difficult to crack.

Occasionally Norman would surprise his large roommate with some observation or idea that had never occurred to Hal. One evening after the boys had turned off the lights, Norman chirped, "You know, Hal, the great thing about college is we, for the first time in our lives, we can go to sleep anytime we want. Just think about it. Throughout our childhood, or at least my early childhood, there was someone telling us when to turn off the lights." Hal recalled, at home, he was often on his own at bedtime, but in the Sewickly dorm, lights out was at 10:00 PM.

"Agree. It is a freedom I sure appreciate even though we are usually lights-out around eleven."

"Yes, Hal, but we can talk all night if we want," came the voice from the nearby bed.

There was quiet as both boys apparently thought about this significant albeit taken-for-granted benefit of being college students. Norman added, "And how fast, abrupt it happens. One minute you're living at home under parents' rules, and the next day, you are forever free to go to bed whenever you choose."

It occurred to Norman that electricity was the key. "Hal, it was less than a century ago when Edison had that eureka moment and invented the electric light. Only then did man become truly free from darkness. Now we can reach over, turn on our desk lights and do so many things that could not have been done a century ago. For many centuries man had only fire on the edge of their home sites. Then candles and whale oil lamps, then electricity. But just think. For centuries mankind lived, worked, or played only when there was sunlight. I never thought about it this way until now. It was the surge in new technology that freed not just us college kids but all mankind from the tyranny of night."

Hal was slowly nodding off, but it was something he had given scant thought to. He sure had a thinking roommate.

Chapter 13

On a bright October Saturday morning with dew on the campus lawn, the boys decided to walk to the Birch River, cross over the old stone bridge near the lumber yard and hike up to the top of a ridge overlooking the town and campus. The crisp air, the river glittering with reflected sunbeams, and the puffy white cumulous clouds merged to produce a vigorous release of shared stories, particularly, as was wont, from Norman Emory.

"My father's roots go all the way back to Scotland's wars of independence with England centuries ago. His great-grandfather came to America in 1865 after his family's cotton business in Manchester was obliterated by cheaper US competition. He built a business in Massachusetts that thrived until our country's textile industry went into a long decline from foreign competition. Irony, yea? Anyway, Hal, my grandparents eventually moved to Pittsburgh, where my grandfather, a big, strong man with white hair, would sit me on his lap and tell stories of the management and labor wars that occurred in the steel industry back in the twenties and thirties. I was five or six, and while I didn't understand everything he talked about, I loved his voice and the warmth of his body.

"He was a union leader. Somehow he lost a finger in

a fight on the job with his shop steward. It was his pinky finger, and he would hold his hand up near mine and say, 'Norman, my boy, touch that stub,' and I reluctantly would. It was awful to feel like octopus tentacles. He would then say, 'Son, this is why you have to get a college education. You don't want to work with your hands, no steel mills or coal mines for my grandson. Right?'

"I would eagerly nod in agreement. Poppy, as I affectionately called him, would then say, 'Cross your heart and hope to die?' And I would cross my heart and speak clearly, as he demanded, 'And I hope to not die.' He would roar with laughter and give me a big hug. I loved that man."

Hal said, "I know something about steel mill work from living in Duquesne. From my house, it often looked like a night at noon. I've breathed enough of that black smoke already. I have seen the workers leaving the steel mills, black faces, grimy hands, straggling with lunchbox in hand, exhausted from ten hours of factory work. It's not for me either, Norman." As they began their climb uphill, Hal added, "And a few miles south of the city across into West Virginia, there are a number of coal mines, and one-day last summer, this guy I worked with at the beer distributor, well not really directly with, we were on different shifts, but anyway he plays football

60

at Pitt and invited me to shoot some hoops with him on a Sunday, our day off. He picked me up in his car, and we played for an hour or two on the outdoor courts at the university. When finished, he said, 'I have to pick up my father. He's working at the mine, doing overtime this week. That's why I have the family car today. You want to come with me? I'll take you home after I drop him off.'

"Long story, but the point is I can still see his father walking in line with co-workers. He looked like one of those soldiers pictured in a trench in the first World War. He had worked all his life underground. And as soon as he got in the car, he lit up a Lucky Strike, and the coughing began. I've seen enough to never want to work labor. I thought I'm going to get my college degree and make a life far from here."

Norman thought this was the most expressive Hal had been. He had actually shared his hopes and dreams, or at least some of them.

"Hal, that's tragic what happens to men who have to endure hard labor. I know you'll succeed in anything you want in life. You have all the tools." And, he was tall, something Norman would never be.

As approaching the top of the ridge, they stopped to take in the ethereal beauty below. Norman thought he would never forget this picture of the serene allure of the surrounding, sloping mountains, the winding river, and the town below. The white steeple of the church on campus stood as a beacon of the bucolic small-town landscape. He wondered if Hal, too, was feeling the pristine nature, its sharp contrast with people everywhere in motion, cars and billboards, city smoke, and the black dust of the steel factories and coal mines.

Sparked by Hal's lucid response, Norman continued his family story.

"Hal, when my dad was about our age, the Great Depression came, and he was unable to afford to go to college. He joined the army, fortunately completing his duty before the Second War. He joined the Pennsylvania State Police, shared an apartment with another officer in McKeesport, and there he met the woman who would become my mom. She was waiting tables at a diner a block or so from where my dad worked. She was living at home and saving money so she could go to college. Well, as things go, they got married, and before she could go to school, she was pregnant with me. I sometimes wonder if she regrets having me." Not wanting to turn their light conversation into a somber mood, he added, 'And now I have a wonderful sister, but that's another story."

Hal stopped suddenly, his gaze fixed ahead. There was a whining sound, an animal-like cry. "Look," he shouted, pointing to a large bird struggling to move about forty yards ahead. Hal darted, Norman trailing, to the spot under a tree where a wild turkey was snared in spring trap with steel jaws clamped down on his legs. The bird must have weighed thirty pounds. Hal kneeled down and examined the trap, and as Norman looked on in stunned dismay, the large boy placed his hands on the opposite edges of the steel trap and pulled. Slowly the trap door opened. Hal picked up the turkey, held it in his arms, rocking it like a baby, and then hastened a few yards off the trail to where the forest of trees began. Norman caught up and watched from behind as Hal, with the slightest thrust of his hand, set the bird free and watched it flutter into the woods. Hal fell to his knees, head down, and didn't move for several seconds. Norman thought he might be praying but said nothing. It was a moment not to be broken by a voice.

Hal looked at his friend and said, "This is enough for today. Let's go back."

They hurriedly retraced their steps down the hilly path and back through town to the dorm. All the while, Hal Sparrow never spoke of the feat. It was like there had been no turkey, no trap, and no release. Like they'd never been to the hill.

Chapter 14

A week or two after the event on the hilltop ridge Norman and Hal were plodding back to the dorm following a one-point Calvin football team loss in the college stadium when they heard a voice behind them. "Calling room 211. Calling room 211. Mutt and Jeff." The boys looked around to see Eddie Carpenter and Johnny Cummings, roommates on the same floor in the dorm.

"Where you guys headed?"

Norman spoke as the two caught up with them. "Back to the dorm. We're analyzing that crap call the blind ref made. "That holding penalty." Hal echoed, "was a killer."

Cummings quipped with a faux smile, "Damn tough loss, but our boys will live to play another game.. We're taking our sorrow to the Old Town Tavern for a jug of the state's finest three-point two brews. Maybe a hard-boiled egg, a frank with chili. Why not join us? Take a break from the prison food."

Cummings was a New Yorker and acted it as though Hal had never met a New Yorker until he arrived at Calvin. Carpenter was from somewhere up that way, New Jersey, maybe. Hal looked at Norman and shrugged his shoulders, like, "It's up to you."

"I've never been there," the smaller boy replied. "What about you, Hal? One beer, maybe? We have been working pretty hard."

"Suckers, if you don't," Cummings retorted.

Carpenter adding, "Come on, what's the big deal? You English majors can rest the books today. It's Saturday. They don't take attendance at the chapel." First-year students were required to take a weekly class in the New Testament and encouraged but not required to attend church on Sundays.

The Old Town Tavern, the only establishment in town that served beer, was located on an unpopulated side street on the ground floor of a two-story clapboard building badly in need of paint. Having a monopoly on publicly served beer, the appearance of the bar didn't seem to bother its owner, nor a local townie crowd and a handful of Calvin male students. Extended over the sidewalk at its entrance was a rusting metal sign with fading red letters wheezing the bar's name. The "O" was barely legible, as were the "V" and "R" in Tavern.

With the insouciance of upperclassmen and the ill-disguised pompousness of a seasoned Prep, Carpenter and Cummings pushed through the door with Hal and Norman following. The boys were met inside by a rush of cigarette smoke and the clamor of voices at the bar, where a handful of male "townies" in wool plaid shirts and baggy overalls were engaged in vigorous dialogue. As the boys stepped to the crowded bar Hal heard the assertive Appalachian dialect of a bearded patron with a pipe in hand, "I'm a wagerin' that'll be the only game we lose all season." Another replied, "Yup, next week we play Clarkston Central. We'll give them a drillin.'" Hal realized they were talking about Lewisburg high school, not the Cougars.

In the corner by the front window were several Preps, mug in one hand and fag in the other, adding to the verbal cacophony and smoke pollution and to The Old Town Tavern's cash register. The burly bartender was leaning over a beer tap filling a quart pitcher. Two other new arrivals were queuing up to attract his attention.

Cummings said, "Follow me," as he weaved his way into the back room with no windows, a dozen tables, all but one unoccupied. Not a woman or girl in sight.

Hal had spent little time in bars. On a few occasions when his mother was not at home, he had been coerced into accompanying his father to a neighborhood saloon. This past summer, he worked in a brewery distributor's warehouse, loading barrels of beer onto trucks and playing for his employer's adult team in the Pittsburgh Summer Outdoor Basketball League. Once or twice after a game, he joined his older teammates at a nearby pub but didn't find beer, particularly to his liking. He'd sip slowly while listening attentively to the happy banter after a win and the regretful grumble after a setback. Having seen the effect of alcohol on his father, he wanted to exorcise himself from its temptation. A teacher at Sewicley said the propensity for a drink is genetically acquired, and that information bolstered his resolve to avoid alcohol.

Norman had said one reason his father wanted him to attend college at Calvin was because of the school's no-alcohol policy. His father, on the job had seen the effects of drunk driving.

"As you know, he's a highway police officer and says many speeders he pulls over have been drinking. And he can cite the number of traffic arrests and deaths in the county caused by booze."

Despite his father's admonition, Norman, with a brush of bravado during a recent night when both found sleep elusive, revealed with an uncharacteristic touch of braggadocio, "I got bombed twice in high school at sleepovers in friend's houses. I can handle a cold one and kind of like the feeling." He paused while thinking about what he had said and added, "My dad would send me packing to the army if he heard this."

What Norman did not say was his father's insistence on his abstinence was because his mother had a problem with alcohol. "A drinking issue," he once heard his father, in an admonishing rebuke, say to his mother. His parents' marriage seemed normal based upon his observation of school pals' families or the radio and then TV program *Father Knows Best*. They got along, he'd thought, and didn't argue much though his father was the dominant one when a disagreement arose over the route of a Sunday drive or what weekend movie the family will see and the restaurant dinner thereafter. It was his mother who had the last say in the attire Norman would wear to church.

Norman knew she drank on certain occasions such as when the Murphys occasionally arrived for dinner with a bottle of red wine in hand or when his father had to stay overnight in Harrisburg for state police meetings. Norman thought maybe it was because she was resentful that she was never able to go to college after his birth. Money was scarce. Two babies in four years was a full-time job. And maybe his mother had a genetic inclination to drink. Would that be inherited?

Hal found the banter of Carpenter and Cummings, doppelgängers if he understood the meaning of the word, tedious, self-centered. Their topic of the moment was their discovery of two "delicious" coeds. Carpenter blustered, they were later meeting two chicks at the CSC. The other said, "You guys must have seen these two chicks always together in skirts halfway between their knees and home plate." Chuckles. "One we call Raccoon because she wears inch-thick eye shadow and a mass of mascara. Has that languid look."

Carpenter interrupted, "Or maybe it's really because she can't sleep thinking of you." Ha, ha.

Hal smiled wanly, and Norman looked around the room to see if he recognized any of the other Calvin boys.

"The other flapper," Cummings again, "name is Eliza, her father's a minister in some state burg I never heard of, and her chest could carry the Library of Congress."

Hal glanced at Norman, pleased to see by his indifferent expression he wasn't interested in prolonging time spent with these smug Preps.

" Yea, you guys have seen them. The Coon has a bundle of long blonde hair and an ass that wiggles when she walks, and the Chest's a redhead who wears her Lucille Ball style with a bird's nest on top. And at the CSC, you can smell her Channel 22 from three booths away."

As Norman and Hal exchanged a quick look, signaling agreement to depart, Carpenter changed the subject.

"Hal, we aren't; well, I'm not really a big basketball fan. I was a wrestler at Hopkins, but hey, I respect what you guys can do with the ball, and I know hoops is the second religion down here. Also, the word is you are the incoming star frosh. All-state PA, huh?"

Hal looked past Carpenter as if a faraway ghost had asked the question, a sign that neither Prep caught, which suggested to Hal neither had any interest in his life.

"Not quite. But Coach told me I could play here. Maybe you'll become a fan." The Preps nodded unconvincingly. Cummings took a deep swallow of the insipid beer and declared, "My sport is shooting cooze, watching it, and thinking what it'd be like to touch, smell, and you know the rest." Carpenter guffawed with a slap on his knee, adding, "Shooting cooze, that's what I hear the moonshine brewers in the hollows call it. Shooting cooze. I love that word." Norman decided not to remind him it was two words. "Can't wait to tell the boys back home this one." Cummings downed his brew.

Carpenter eased out of his chair, "Good seeing you, Shakespeare scholars. Drink with moderation. We're off."

"Stay well, " Norman said without rising from his seat.

Norman said, "Some of these guys from the East are assholes. These guys are too, but harmless, I say." Hal nodded, wondering what they would major in, and thought neither would have to worry about finding a job after school even if they didn't graduate. Their daddies would find one for them. He had known boys like this at Sewickly.

Hal said, "Are you ready, roomie?" The foursome had consumed two pitchers on average, three glasses a piece, and even the watered-down stuff in that quantity had some kick. Norman said, "Let's have a hot dog and a hard-boiled egg and one more pitcher. We'll take it slowly. Nothing to do tonight anyway."

Hal guessed Norman, such a small guy was probably a bit tipsy but decided not to be a spoilsport and negate one more refill. After all the alcohol content was 3.2% half that in Pennsylvania beer. Hal had seen enough of what an excess of booze could do, and here was Norman, who had also seen the impact of drink in his home, now wanting more. It had to be genetic, Hal thought, reminding himself that he would beat any genetic urge to become a victim of alcohol.

Norman was right about one thing there was nothing else to do unless it was going to the CSC. They were on top of homework finished in the library before kickoff. Hal didn't pose an objection. They had seldom been off campus.

"Hal, you know I know sports. I love to watch games and write about them. But I envy you for being able to

71

play a sport well and at the college level. I must have been doing something else when God was handing out tall bodies." A sign of the impact of the beer?

He smiled wistfully and continued. "It must be so thrilling to be able to race up and down the floor, to leap sky high and grab a rebound. I could only imagine the feeling a player has when he is introduced to the crowd by the PA announcer or when he goes to the foul line knowing thousands of eyes are on him."

Hal nodded unconvincingly like it was no big deal and a lot of work.

Norman went to the bar and returned with two hot dogs. Hal had never had a frank with chili on it and doubted Norman had. In Pittsburgh, hot dogs came with chopped onions and lots of mustard. Realizing they'd missed dinner at the dorm, he finished his though it lacked the juicy taste of the dogs they sold at Forbes Field or at Anthony's Bar and Grill in Duquesne. Hal thought it wasn't like prison food, as one of the Preps had said about the meals in the dorm and, by implication, all foods south of the Mason-Dixon line. In a change of subject, Norman mentioned he had seen this raccoon girl somewhere in the halls of a classroom building.

It was then Hal asked Norman if he had a girlfriend back home. "Not at the moment. Do you?"

Hal reminded him attending an all-boys school and

living the last three summers in the home of family friends of Sewickly made it difficult to meet girls and date. "And I don't have a car."

The room at The Old Town Tavern was beginning to empty as more students headed to the door. Norman had finished the hot dog, sat back, and said, "Hal, I've been meaning to ask you. I know you have told me a little about it, and I feel awful for you," having hesitated for a moment, " but what happened with your Mom and Dad? I mean, I know you said they're divorced but do you see them? Do you write? Do they? Not trying to meddle; I only ask because, well, I care about you."

Norman forced a nervous smile attempting to lighten the directness of his question. Yes, he realized Hal had mentioned during their late-night chats that his father had left home, but immediately after this comment, the larger boy had become quiet, and Norman chose not to push for more information. Sitting here, his queries were likely aided by the emboldening effect of the beer.

Hal looked into the beer's blond flush as if it held some insight into what went wrong with his parents. He leaned back in his chair. "Yes, it's OK, Norman." While he was not enthusiastic to again go through his life story, he valued his growing friendship with his roommate and decided the boy's sincerity and sensitivity deserved a more detailed response.

"My father, "Big Bird" Sparrow, he was called by those barflies he hung out with, was and still is, to my knowledge, a bad drinker. He grew up in Pittsburgh, had gone to Slippery Rock College on a football scholarship, and according to my mother, who met him there while she was still in high school, they fell in love and married the day after she graduated. He got a job selling ads in the county Yellow Pages and then a better job selling space at the Allegheny County newspaper." Hal paused his gaze now in distant contemplation. Norman almost said, "I know that paper, excellent local journalism," but wisely thought it might derail Hal's interest in continuing.

"Anyway, he was supposedly doing pretty good. He can bullshit with the best of them, and before they knew it, she was pregnant. My two sisters, born a year apart, Elaine and Suzanne, are nine and eight years older than me, and both were out of the house by the time I was ten or eleven.

"I was too young to know what really happened, but I think he got fired from his job. Something happened that apparently damaged any ambition he had for work, and things got worse. And now I don't see him anymore."

Hal paused, having told this story so often it seemed he could deliver it from memory, but if anyone he knew who wanted and deserved to hear it was Norman. Hal recalled the first time he told it. He was being interviewed by Sewickly's headmaster, Mr. Edward DePugh. The private prep school each year took in a dozen students, mostly good athletes whose families lacked the financial support to enable their sons to attend. Hal was one of those accepted that year. He was nervous that day as he carefully replayed to the headmaster the disintegration of his parents' marriage and the most recent tragedy. The second time, a week later, the words came easier. He was taken to meet Mr. and Mrs. Nelson, a wealthy childless couple who lived near the school. The husband was a successful attorney, and an alumnus of Sewickly, and his wife taught English there. They liked him and told Mr. DePugh they would seek court approval for Hal to live with them in the summers while he attended Sewickly and lived in the dormitory. This plan, a new life for Hal, one he happily agreed to, had to be approved by the state of Pennsylvania. After a day of testimony of a court-appointed child psychiatrist and a city sociologist, both of whom agreed with the plan, and with the ringing support of Mr. DePugh and Mr. and Mrs. Nelson, the judge granted the request. Hal would live with the Nelsons when not boarding at the school. The Nelsons were happy and loving people and treated him like a son. Mr. DePugh lived up to his promise, meeting for an hour every other week with Hal counseling him on academics, and listening to how he was feeling about life in general. If any doubted his adjustment to life without parents and in a new school with challenging academics, Hal Sparrow proved them wrong. He blossomed in the environment, mature enough to realize he had been given a lifetime opportunity to shape his future.

The last time Hal told the story, it sounded as if he were listening to someone else's voice. It was when Coach Andrews from Calvin came to Sewickly and had lunch with Mr. DePugh and him. At the end of the meeting, Coach Andrews offered Hal a full scholarship.

"Norman, be back in a moment. Bathroom call." While Hal was gone, Norman drained his glass and refilled it halfway from what was left in the pitcher. One more, he thought. First college beer and how good it was to have it with roomie Hal. He could talk to him, reveal his thoughts, speak about anything. In their room, they talked about Introduction to "American Literature," one of two classes they shared, and the other "Contemporary Language Structure." Although Hal had not read as extensively as his roommate, he was willing to listen, to question, and to learn. Norman had read Homer's Iliad and Odyssey and some Shakespeare, Milton, and Moliere. Hal had written his senior English paper at Sewicley on *Moby Dick.* Attending the same two classes together and after dinner discussions about both spurred increasingly more discussion, shared insights, and challenging new questions with the added benefit of creating a larger, personal, and at times, a more intimate bond between the two. Norman felt he had the perfect roommate: a basketball star-to-be with interest in literature and learning. He could be very helpful to this boy whose life had been hard, help him with his studies, and be there when he wanted to talk about his life, like now.

Hal, returning to the table, was thinking about how quickly his life was changing. The environment was so different here in Lewisburg from Sewickly and his Duquesne neighborhood in downtown Pittsburgh. Being here in this unfamiliar and diverse environment seemed to make it easier to forget the past and with Nelson to talk about it. He felt comfortable telling Norman more about his life pre-Calvin.

Norman was finishing a sip from his nearly empty glass. "Hal, I'm glad we came here." Hal nodded unconvincingly, sensing that was not the way a 100% sober Nelson would say it.

"Well, to finish my story. With my sisters gone, both married and living somewhere out of the area, my mother, who had got her college degree at night before I was born, began substitute teaching, a day-to-day thing.

There were few full-time teaching jobs available, and they went to fresh-out-of-school teachers who, by union rules, were paid less than my mother. Meanwhile, my father was bouncing from job to job, selling storm windows, vacuum cleaners, and encyclopedias door-to-door jobs on commission, with no salary. His white-collar days selling ads were over. With no more full-time employment, his drinking increased. There were times three or four straight days when he didn't come home. Didn't call, and then suddenly, he'd appear through the front door with a wide smile upon his ruddy face acting as if nothing had happened. And he'd spread his arms wide as if he were Jesus welcoming us into his flock. 'Greetings, everybody. Papa's home. Is everybody happy?' as grinned as if he were happy to be home. At first, I believed he was being honest and was interested in us; how we were. But I began to understand he was just mocking us. My mother would ask him for money, but he always said he would have some tomorrow or next week. She finally found a full-time teaching job, but it was an hour away across the river in Ohio. Then one day, I was in seventh grade, and in my room when I heard him yelling he wouldn't pay some bill owed. Said she owed him for all the years he was the sole supporter, that kind of rubbish. She went wild with rage. She accused him of keeping some floozy, told him to pack his clothes and leave, and threatened to change the locks on the door. She said she had had enough of his philandering, his drinking, and freeloading. I opened the door thinking, I guess seeing me might somehow calm them down. It did for the moment. Both stopped and looked at me, and somehow I was able to say to him, 'Please don't go.'

"She said, 'Stay out of this, Norman. Go to your room. I will handle this.' I remember it like it was yesterday. Moments later, I peeked out to see him going out the door. No goodbyes to either of us. Didn't even close the door."

Hal took another sip of beer as Norman watched, spellbound, hearing a version of a life he had never imagined.

"But on occasion, he would come back. She never got around to having the locks changed. Sometimes I think she actually wanted him to be able to get in the house. Maybe because she could release her emotions. We never talked about it, though. My mom wasn't much of a talker, and I never wanted to upset her with questions about the situation.

"Then, one night, I heard her scream. I jumped out of bed and ran to the living room, where I saw them glaring at each other like two prizefighters waiting for the bell to ring. She yelled, "James Edward Sparrow, You're a lazy, no good liar. Can't keep a job. You bully our son because you're jealous of him. He's smarter than you, and he has a future. You squandered your future, and though you'd never admit it, it's true, and you hate it."

"Enough, Emily. You're a broken record. A woman who wishes she was a man and because you're not, you hate men. And you never cared about our two daughters. Never went to Carly's soccer games. Never praised Beth for being on the honor roll every fucking semester." He laughed.

"And you, Mister Big Shot, are really a dumb ass. Couldn't even finish college taking those Mickey Mouse courses...."

"That's enough, Emily. God damn it, I mean it. And since Hal's home, hiding in his bedroom, listening to your hysterical rant, I want him to hear something he's never heard before. Something I never told him because I didn't want our boy to hear the truth about his mother. The perfect wife and mother. Bullshit. I'm going to give him a little history lesson because you're behaving like the mean, nasty bitch you are." She left the room and slammed the bedroom door.

"'Son, you should know when your mother saw me, she thought of nothing else except getting me to the alter. She knew every trick in the book. She was in need of a husband, of someone to pay her college bills, a man to support her through life. She was like a hungry cat in pursuit of a mouse. And chased me around.'"

"He continued bitching about something bad about her when she returned to the room, her face red, fists clenched. I saw daggers in her eyes and knew there was going to be a bad fight.

"'You're the one to talk,' she said. 'you never cared for either one of them. You know damn well, Jim, you don't like women. You're terrified of them. Why? Because you are a weak man James Sparrow. You can't support a family and hate me because I'm no longer supporting you. You have failed in every half ass job you ever had.'"

At that moment, he strode across the room and slapped her face. I don't know if I even said anything. I was like insane. I ran towards him, fists clenched with the aim to strike him. I took a swing which he blocked and hit me with a hard blow on my ear. Then he was gone."

"Jesus, Hal," Norman lamented. "I'm so sorry. Really awful stuff."

"We didn't see him for weeks. There was peace in the house. She seemed happy he was gone though she didn't say that. I could see it in her smile, hear it in the tone of her voice. I'd arrive home after practice, and we would have peaceful dinners. We didn't have a television, so I would do my homework, then read the *Gazette*'s sports section, and in the baseball season, listen to Pirates night games on KDKA. Then after months of this, I guess you would call it stability with shared time between us, she began not coming home for dinner. She said she had met some nice people at the school where she was teaching. It was a long drive, and when the weather was bad, it took even longer for her to get home.

"Then, one evening, I was alone in the living room listening to a Duquesne game on KDKA radio when he walked in the door. Without a word, he went to the kitchen and returned with a glass of whiskey in hand.

"Where the hell is she? Dirty dishes in the sink, crap on the floor. Meanwhile, we know damn well where she is out sleeping with her latest lover. She's let us down, son. Me and you and the girls who left us at their first opportunity. It has to be said she's a selfish one. I needed a drink and went to the kitchen and found, no shit surprise; there was less than an inch left in the bottle of Jim Beam. Someone's been sneaking it when I'm not around. And I don't think it's you because you know I'd whip your ass if it were. Could I be wrong?' I said maybe so, one of the first times I ever 'talked back" to him. That was the term he had used several times before, 'don't you never talk back to me, son.' As soon as the words left my mouth, I was in for some trouble.

He looked at me square in the eyes for what seemed a long moment and said, 'Maybe so, huh? You're getting real learning in school, huh? 'I'll tell you what. Real learning comes not in some classrooms. It comes from the streets, out there with real people, not words written in books or listening to canned voices of teachers or the talk radio dunces who never had work or to fight for anything.' It somehow occurred to me he had never mentioned being in Korea, where there was real fighting. I think, Norman, that was because of some injury he had from football.

"I long ago realized arguing with him was no good. He either berated me further or gestured a threatening slap in the face. So I had usually kept quiet. "

Norman swayed back in his chair. His empathy for Hal was infinite.

"Then, and let me sum this up, Norman. Time to head back to the dorm. A few months later, my mother began not coming home from work a day or two a week. She said she was staying with a friend from work who lived closer to the school. I knew something was going on. She was changing her mood, becoming more distracted, and less interested in my classes in my sports. Meanwhile, I was by now in eighth grade, six-two, one-sixty-five. One day I came home after a basketball game we had lost. I was in a bad mood, and all I wanted was to have a bowl of soup and go to bed. There he was, sitting on the couch, feet up on the table, reading the paper. He looked up with a self-satisfied grin on his unshaven face and a bottle of beer in hand.

"'What are you looking so pissed off about?' he growled.

"I shrugged my shoulders, looked away, and walked to my room. A little later, I went to the kitchen, hoping to find some dinner. He was now approaching me.

"'You think life is tough. Had a bad day in school. Teacher yell at you. Maybe got your ass beat at practice or played a bad game. Let me tell you, son. You don't know the half of it.' That was one of his favorite expressions: You don't know the half of it.' Like he knew a hundred percent of it. 'Life gets tougher every day, young man. You got it good now, and don't forget it.'

"I found a can of soup and was opening it when I heard the front door slam shut. In walked my mother. Then it began. Same stuff. 'What the hell are you doing here, you bum? You did this' 'No, you said that. No, you never gave a good shit about anybody other than yourself. You're a liar.' All that stuff, Norman." Hal wondered why he didn't call his roommate Norm easier, one syllable less. He might, from now on.

"Next thing I knew, he struck her hard, and she bounced off the living room wall. I can still hear the thumping sound. I snapped. I honestly can't recall any thoughts going through my head. In the next instant, I was up behind him and grabbed his shoulder. He spun around, and I cold-cocked him. My right hand, a short windup, nailed him right in the jaw. I can still hear the sound, the smack of bone against bone. I felt the pain in my hand and my wrist mostly. He fell straight back like a toy soldier knocked over in slow motion and hit the floor out cold. I thought, at first, I might have killed him. My mother started screaming incoherently, got to her feet, and struggled into her bedroom. I called, 'Mom. Mom, are you OK?' She said, 'Go to your room. I want to be alone.'

"Instead, I was really frightened; I ran out to Lucas Jankowski's house on the next block, a teammate whose parents knew about the situation at home. I told them my parents were having a talk and needed privacy, and they let me spend the night.

"Well, a long story short: my mother found a lawyer who went to court and got a restraining order against my father. He was not allowed to see either of us for six months. That was a relief, and life returned to normalcy. Soon I learned she, as I suspected, had a new man-friend. She brought him home one day, and he seemed nice enough, a widower with two kids. Sometime afterwards, he proposed marriage after her divorce. Then one day, I was in eighth grade, my teacher said the principal wanted to see me after class in his office. A uniformed police officer was sitting next to thc principal. 'Please have a seat, son. There is some bad news.' The officer looked down at me and said, 'There has been a terrible accident. We tried to find a relative to speak with you but couldn't locate one. Your mother died a couple of hours ago in an automobile accident. I am very sorry.'

"And that was it, Norman. She was hit walking across an icy street a block from the school where she taught by a car driven by a kid who got his driver's license a couple of weeks before. Both parents; gone. My sisters had made lives for themselves and had no interest in taking me in. I stayed with the Jankowski's for a few weeks until the court decided I would have to live in the city's orphanage, Boys Town, as you probably have heard of it until I got adopted, which was no slam dunk, or until I turned eighteen and finished high school. My coach wanted to keep me at his house through high school, but he had three kids, and the judge determined I would be better off at this orphanage.

"Soon thereafter, my coach DePugh of Sewickly came to school to meet me. He then got the Nelsons involved and persuaded the court I would have a better life attending school at Sewickly and living with the Nelsons in the summers. All this took four or five months, but life at Sewickly was good. And here I am. Here we are, Norman. Time to head back to the dorm. I'm getting sleepy."

"But what about your father?"

"Have no idea. Not something I think about."

Chapter 15

There was something Hal didn't tell Norman, something so tragic that he caused or didn't prevent from happening. Something so recent, so troubling, he had told no one. It occurred three months ago in his summer job. An alumnus of Sewickly, Ed Townsend, owned a beer distribution business in Crafton Heights near where the Allegheny and Monongahela rivers meet to form the Ohio River. He was an avid basketball fan who seldom missed a game and a good friend of Hal's coach. Townsend often visited the locker room when the team triumphed over a longtime rival to congratulate the coach and players. It was after the first season tournament game in March when Townsend approached Hal and offered him summer employment. His primary job was to sweep the floor of the forty-thousand square foot warehouse, empty the trash cans, and lend a hand to the full-time workers who loaded, unloaded, and stacked the kegs and cases of Fort Pitt, Duquesne, and Iron City, the three regional beers. The largest of these stainless steel kegs was twenty-four inches high, contained fifty gallons of beer, weighed one hundred and forty pounds, and had to be set atop another in a refrigerated locker room. Most of the beer in the warehouse, however, was in cases of cans and bottles and had to be stacked on a platform known as a pallet. Each pallet contained ninety-eight cases, nearly reaching the forty-foot high ceiling. There were rows after rows of perfectly aligned pallets distanced three feet from each other. The Three River Distribution Company warehouse had a dozen motorized forklifts with a pronged device in front for lifting and carrying the cases operated by seasoned employees. Every morning the forklifts would deliver the designated number of cases to the ramp, where the three-man crew of the particular truck readied to deliver the beer to the retail outlets it served. Throughout the day, the trucks would return with empty kegs and bottles, and often the crew would reload and repeat the same process.

Hal was the only high school summer employee though he had just graduated from Sewickly. There were two college guys who worked there, one of whom was Townsend's son, the other a football player at Pitt. They each worked either different shifts or in different areas of the warehouse, so Hal didn't have much time to get to know them through the Pitt guy, and he occasionally played outdoor basketball after work. He did, however, get to know the three guys who were assigned to the pallets in his location, guys he worked with every day.

Sparky was a dream employee. Never late, always willing to lend a hand to a fellow worker, never critical of management, and an important voice in persuading others to vote against a Teamster campaign to unionize.

He was generally quiet, precise in his brief use of language, a contemplative man whose job it was to inspect the on-and-off-loading of cases on the forklift to ensure successful stacking. A thin and wiry man in his early forties who had five young children, of whom he would occasionally mention his pride in their academic achievements. "You can bet all of them will graduate from high school, and half, maybe even all, will go on to college," he claimed, and no one doubted him.

There was something Sparky kept to himself, a secret from his fellow workers. He was taking classes two nights a week at Allegheny Community College on the way to getting his college degree. He didn't want to tell the guys at work because that might jinx the whole thing, and a guy like 2G would probably rag on him. Call him a fink. Sparky was making up for a misspent youth of pool-sharking, running numbers for Hebert, the Horse, and dropping out of high school to join the Navy before the arm of the law caught him. He'd get an education, by God, he told himself every day when he headed for his evening class at the community college. And he was damn committed; his kids would too.

Giuseppe Gerabaldi, or "G2," as everyone called him, was only a few years older than Hal and had been voted the Pittsburgh high school football player of the year back in '54. What Hal learned at work was G2's dreams of playing fullback in front of family and friends for the Pitt University Panthers ended suddenly when in the last game of his scholastic career, he took a helmet-to-helmet blow from a massive OhioState-bound linebacker and was stretchered off the field. The diagnosis: no future football. The university pulled the scholarship offer, and G2 bummed around the neighborhood bars doing some part-time work at the mills.

G2 was a bachelor who enjoyed his cups at any one of a number of going-nowhere local taverns often populated with a collection of other local one-time sports legends who'd never lived up to their high school billings and today were on the other side of yesterday. Occasionally after his shift, he would have a beer or two on-premise with Sparky and Oldie, the third guy in Hal's section, where he would regale his fellow workers with tales of past gridiron heroics and his recent triumphs with "tasty tarts on the make." He fashioned himself as a ladies' man with irresistible charm. "I don't mean to sound cocky, but I gotta beat 'em off....they do the coming-on, I do the comin' off." He boasted of victorious barroom brawls with "morons" looking for trouble by delivering an upper right fist to their chin. "Motherfucker messes with me; he's messin' with the wrong motherfucker." His modus operandi when it came to broads or brawls was "Make the first move. Strike the morons quickly and charm the broads with sweet malarkey. Move on."

The other guy Hal worked with was "Oldie," John O'Malley in his early fifties, who revealed with pride his nickname was bestowed by his wife, Honey, twenty years his junior. It was a spurious epithet suggesting their age difference, but its real meaning was quite the opposite. "I'm a stud, hung like a horse. Honey tells me I make love like the way that movie star James Dean must do it. She says I'm really a youngster in the sack, which is why she calls me Oldie. She don't want none of her women friends to know she's got a feisty jackrabbit at home. Says she never trusts females. They're like cats, she says."

Oldie was the crew's forklift driver in Hal's section and the de facto boss of the group when an unexpected decision had to be made. He was serious every moment during his shift behind the wheel of a forklift, carefully guiding it through the narrow rows of their warehouse with its overhanging pallets holding enough beer to flood the Ohio River. Not once in his eighteen years had Oldie had an accident with his vehicle, never even made the slightest contact with the towering stacks, something not every Townsend driver could say. When the work day ended, he would call Honey from the pay phone in the warehouse and let her know he would be having a beer or two with the boys but not to worry; her jackrabbit would be home before she jumped in the sack.

*   *   *

There was a trivial but pleasant benefit of working at Three Rivers Distribution Company, one that all the guys in the warehouse could partake in. It happened, well, not really "happened" because Mr. Townsend made it so. There was a vending machine located near the bathroom room that, for a nickel, delivered a can of Coca-Cola or Sprite, or for a dime, scout's honor, the employees could purchase a cold beer in a damaged can. Such cans were there because in the distribution process, there were occasional "drops," when a case might tumble off the truck while loading or unloading the forklift, and the cans would be dented by the impact. The company could not deliver cans in such condition to their customers, so Mr. Townsend figured a way to generate some revenue from the drops and, in the process, buck up employee morale. A can of Fort Pitt in neighborhood bars costs thirty cents, and the boys at work could buy a dented one in the warehouse's cooler for a nickel. There was, however, a rule that an employee could not purchase a beer until the warehouse closed at 6 PM. Anyone seen drinking beer prior would be terminated, with no excuses, no hearing. So on occasion, after working overtime, Hal's crew enjoyed a can or two of "suds," as they called it.

One late afternoon Oldie was beckoned to report to the main office, where the general manager told him two trucks with empty kegs and bottles would be arriving later than expected. He returned to his group with the news. "The boss would like us to work an hour or two overtime. Anyone got a problem with that?"

They all stayed and unloaded the trucks when they arrived, working efficiently as the team they were. Even Hal was allowed to pitch in rolling empty kegs and lifting cases that needed to be placed and cleaned in the morning. He liked this work better than his "no job," as he referred to it, sweeping the floor, emptying and hosing down the trash cans, and filling the vending machine cooler with colas and unsaleable brews. Oldie did his usual first-rate job of angling the forklift through the aisles, between the pallets, and working the mast, the vertical assembly that raises and lowers the side-shifter that allows the operator to move the forks and backrest laterally.

It was after eight when they finished and were the only employees remaining in the warehouse. The warehouse had the quiet feeling of a losing team's dressing room before 2G dug into his pockets and pulled out a handful of change. "Who's got some dimes? It's

Monday, and I got nuthin' to do. Let's have a beer or two to celebrate the overtime dough we just earned."

Oldie looked at his watch. "I already called my child bride, so I'm game. What about you, Sparky?"

"Nah, I want to get home and see if my kids are doing' their homework." He allowed a short chuckle to show the guys it was no big deal like I don't have to be home. I'm not pussy-whipped or anything like that; just something I want to do.

Oldie responded, "Hey, Sparky, give her a call. You know where the pay phone is," flipping him a dime. "Tell her we worked our asses off today, and you'll be a little late. Do you good? And speak to the kids and tell them you'll check their homework in the morning."

Sparky thought about it. He didn't have a class this evening, and he would have missed it by now anyway. It had been a while since he had a little after-work time with the boys. There was something to be said about socializing with your peers. Not always good; being a party pooper, especially when you liked the guys, needed their help and cooperation. He trudged off to the pay phone, which hung on the wall near the vending machine.

G2 looked at Hal. "Here's two quarters, kid. Get us five brews, Iron City, if there are some." Hal wanted to get home which meant hitchhiking a ride the five miles to Sewickly, but he could hardly fink out now. Getting a lift was no easy thing after a rush hour, but he said nothing and fetched the beers.

There were several picnic tables off the main floor, away from the rows of pallets near the boss' office, where guys could take a break and have lunch and a Coke. No one was around now, so the four of them sat down and rewarded themselves with beer that tasted just fine in dented cans.

"One more," G2 said. No one offered an objection. Oldie said, "Kid, you know how to play Liars Poker?"

Hal shook his head.

G2 said, "We'll show you. I got four singles. Oldie, Spark, what's ya got?"

Hal learned that evening, Liars Poker was a game similar to poker but played with dollar bills instead of cards. Simply stated, the winner of a hand is he who bids the highest number of a specific number that is located on the lower left and upper right of all paper dollar bills. No players knows the numbers on any bill except their own. Say a player takes the bid with a bet of eight 2s. He might have, say, only two 2s on his bill, and in this case, he is betting the other, say, three players have a combined six or more 2s. If so, he wins and takes all players' bills. If the total numbers revealed after the bidding ends total less than eight 2s, the bidder loses and pays all players a dollar. If the total number of 2s is revealed to be, eight or more, the bidder wins a dollar from each player. This game is called Liars Poker because a player might have many or none of the number he bids, thus "lying" with the hope the other players have enough of his bidded number to win the hand. A "hand," or game, could be over in less than a minute with three or four experienced players in the game.

Hal was fascinated watching the bidding process, but when invited to play, he politely refused. Money, a rare item, was not to be risked in a frivolous way.

Sparky stood up, "I've got to be heading home, boys. It's nearly nine."

Oldie said, "Yeah, good idea. Let me finish my beer, and we'll all leave together. I'll lock up."

G2 said, "Oldie, you know I always wanted to do one thing here at work. Something I've never done, and you can make it happen. Five minutes is all it will take."

"Now, what would that be, G?" Oldie was finishing his third beer by Hal's count. G2 was at least even while Sparky was nursing his second.

"Oldie, I want to get behind the wheel of the forklift and feel what it's like to be you. To be able to take it down an aisle and back. Maybe one swing around the floor."

Oldie took a swig of beer. "It ain't no fun, G. It's

work, takes concentration," something Hal thought G2 was short on. "You're not missing anything, G. Let's go home after one more hand." He looked over at Sparky. "One hand and we're outta here." Hal had to pee, and this was the perfect excuse to say goodbye and hit the road. He ambled to the bathroom, thinking he would make his exit in a minute or two, no more procrastination.

G2, feeling perhaps the sense of self-entitlement he claimed to feel in the taverns he frequented, was not hesitant to speak up for what he thought was fair, which meant something he wanted.

"Tell you what, Oldie, one more hand, just you and me. If I win, I get to drive the forklift. If you win, I'll pay you a dollar. That's how bad I want to take the drive."

Oldie looked him in the eye. G2 was a good employee. Oldie liked him, knew his life hadn't been easy having his football future stolen by an illegal clip, and despite G2's claiming he was a magnet to women of any age who would lift their skirts after a first smooch, Oldie heard from Mr. Townsend that G2 lived at home with his sick mother.

Maybe let him get behind the wheel, take it up and back, fifty-a-hundred yards or so. No one around to see it.

"OK, G2, I'm doin' this one time for you. Forget another hand of Liars and no more beer. I'd just relieve you from your George Washingtons anyway and leave you heartbroken. Let's go."

Oldie looked over at Sparky and said in a low voice, "I need your help to keep an eye on our pal."

They followed Oldie and G2 to the twenty yards or so where the forklift was parked.

Oldie spent a minute or two explaining to him how to operate the forklift. "Listen up now, Giuseppe," using his first name to emphasize the seriousness of what he was about to say. "This forklift can travel at speed up to fifteen miles an hour, but company policy is not to exceed eight, and that means never pushing the foot pedal to the floor. I'll be watching, and if you speed up, the game's over, and we're out of here. Five minutes and I'll be clocking you all the way."

There was nothing too tricky about it Oldie thought again. G2 had only to sit in the cab, take the wheel, step on the pedal lightly, steer, and then foot on the brake to stop. He wouldn't be doing any maneuvers with the mast since he had no idea how that worked. Oldie assured himself there was nothing complex about the endeavor.

G2 climbed into the seat as Oldie turned the switch to start the motor. "Keep it slow, G. I'm trusting you."

G2 pulled the gear knob down, and the vehicle began

to move. Off it went at a cautious speed well within the limit Oldie had demanded. G2 turned his head back at his three co-workers and gave them a winning smile with one arm raised in a triumphant manner as the forklift disappeared around the last pallet forty yards down the aisle.

Sparky spoke up. "You sure, Oldie, this is a good idea. He's a little wild, we all know?" Oldie nodded. Sparky feeling the buzz of the suds, wondered if Oldie was influenced by the same.

Hal watched with interest like it was an athletic event, some individual sport, thinking anything could happen if G2 got a little overconfident. He'd heard a rumor that once a forklift slipped suddenly on the surface and slid perilously, bumping into another forklift that suddenly appeared at an intersection of the aisles. He didn't know what to think about G2's braggadocio of female conquests, claims of multiple football scholarship offers from major colleges, and how he was feared when entering any bar in his tough neighborhood. Hal had briefly considered chiming in with Sparky about the possibility of something going wrong with G2 at the helm of the forklift, but he was a part-timer, and they don't make waves.

Off went the forklift turning right again at the far end of the aisle. Oldie smiled, thinking he'd done a good thing and in a minute or two, G2 would be back, and they'd call it a day, but first, he had to pee, couldn't hold it anymore. "Be back in sixty, guys. Nature calling."

Hal and Sparky stood near a pallet, and the older man said, "You're a smart guy Sparrow. Get that college degree, and you'll never have to see the inside of a warehouse again. Get yourself a white-collar job, have lunch in restaurants with waitresses and drive a good car to work. The future, Hal, is in front of you."

Hal smiled, "Thanks, Sparky; I think what you are doing with your kids, helping them with their studies and their homework is a terrific thing. Your kids are really lucky to have you."

Sparky smiled. It meant something that this smart college-bound young man had heard him speak of his kids and acknowledged it now.

It was at that moment they heard the squealing tires and then the impact of a collision. The sound of falling cases.

Sparky began running towards the aisle. Hal wasn't sure what to do: go get Oldie or follow Sparky. He decided to alert Oldie and headed off in a run to the men's room.

Sparky reached the end of the aisle, but the forklift was not in sight. He ran down to the next aisle and looked in both directions, but no forklift. "Hey, G2, where in hell are you, damn it?" he shouted. Running full speed, he reached the fourth aisle and saw the forklift. There were a dozen cases on the floor, broken glass, and flowing suds but luckily nothing more, the pallets built to take collision. What was disturbing was the sight of 2G attempting to turn the forklift around and head back in the direction he had come, in the direction where Sparky stood aghast at the sight.

Hal hesitated, thinking Oldie would have heard the collision and would in, any second, be running this way. He turned and ran down the aisle, where he saw the forklift steaming towards Sparky. Unless G2 could stop the forklift or alter its course, a near impossibility given the width of the aisle, there would be an accident, maybe a terrible one. Why didn't Sparky move from the middle of the aisle, sidle up against a pallet to avoid the coming collision? Or retreat and run away from the forklift?

Hal watched in dread for an instant before yelling, "Sparky, dodge it! Dodge it!" It was too late. The forklift veered into another pallet, and this time, cases of bottled beer began falling near Sparky, breaking on the floor; broken glass, bottle caps, and rivulets of golden fluids began a slow flow. G2 must have panicked, and instead of stepping on the brake, he hit the pedal and skidded into Sparky, who was on the floor covering his head with folded arms trying to avoid the cascade of falling beer cans and bottles. Hal ran towards the collision, slipping on the stream of beer and stopping as he saw a half of Sparky's chest underneath the front tire of the forklift. G2 was jumping up and down, screaming, "Mother of God! Help me!"

Oldie arrived, then the ambulance. It was too late. They'd lost Sparky.

Hal Sparrow has thought about it daily ever since. Had he been indecisive? Should he have stayed with Sparky instead of wasting valuable seconds running to the restroom to get Oldie? He could have helped Sparky. He could have run to the forklift, got there first, and stopped 2G from attempting to turn it around. It likely wouldn't have changed things, but who could ever be sure, Oldie said to him days later, but Hal knew he failed to deliver when needed. When the moment came for him to perform, he wasn't up for it. Life wasn't basketball.

That night Hal cried himself to sleep. There would be no Sparky at work tomorrow, and what would happen to his five kids he loved so much.

Chapter 16

It was dark when Hal and Norman left the smoky back room of the Old Town Tavern. In the moonless sky, a platoon of milky cumulus clouds drifted by in slow motion. Norman miss-stepped a time or two treading the sidewalks of East Main Street as they sauntered back towards campus. Hal thought Norman had a couple of glasses of beer too many, and he should have cut him off before the last pitcher. Should haves were intruding on his post high school life.

Hal was thinking how deserted the street was on this Saturday, October evening, when Norman spoke, "I really feel for you, for the hell you've been through." He stopped, and Hal thought maybe Norm had forgotten something at the bar or was maybe sick. The smaller boy looked up at him with a face of vacillation, thinking of what to say or whether to say it. Hal had never seen his roommate flummoxed like this.

"Hal, I need to tell you about the worst thing that has happened in my life, something that really bothers me. Would you like to hear it?"

"Are you feeling OK, Norman?"

"Yea, I'm feeling a little blitzed but more sad, very sad. I read we drink to escape, to hide unpleasant memories but it's also drinking that makes the mind remember the things we'd like to forget. I want to tell you something no one down here knows."

"Sure, shoot, buddy."

Hal stopped under the street lamp and watched the lump in Norman's throat bulge as he tried to swallow.

"I told you how important my little sister Carrie is to me, how much I love her. She's four years younger and not so little anymore. One day when she was six, I almost ruined her life. She has still not recovered from it. I have awful dreams about what happened, how I screwed up, a most serious screw-up. I see her terrified face in my nightmares."

It was obvious that Norman was finding it difficult it to say what the "it" was, what happened. "Sorry, Norman, but what was it?"

"Hey, Hal, I shouldn't have brought this up. Compared to having your father leaving and your mother dying unexpectedly, my situation is..."

"Come on; I want to hear. Our awful experiences, regardless of how painful they are or not compared to someone else's, are just as hurtful to each of us."

They reached the intersection of Lumber Street, where a large antebellum house, once the residence of a wealthy lumber baron, now a funeral home, took up half the block. There was no light or sign of life inside. It reminded Hal of his mother's funeral attended by his sisters and their husbands and several people from the school. Hal was unexpectedly asked by the pastor to say a few words, and he did, but afterward he thought of many things forgotten he should have said.

Norman continued. "Not far from our house was a creek which in the spring became almost as wide as the Monongahela. In the summer, it shriveled up to half its size. At the time, I was ten, nearly eleven years old. I had read Edgar R. Burroughs's book *Tarzan of the Apes*. It was also, as you may recall, a comic strip in the Sunday newspaper. I loved Tarzan. He did good things to help natives in danger. He saved animals in trouble and was a good husband to Jane and father to Boy. But what I really thought was neat was how Tarzan swung through the jungle on tree vines from place to place and up to his tree house."

Norman stopped. "This sounds like shit, like I am reporting this, like I am writing a goddamn newspaper article. Who gives a shit about Tarzan or these details? I don't! Maybe I'm just trying to avoid saying what happened! I'll finish this some other time, Hal. I'm fucked."

Hal put his hand on the smaller boy's shoulder. "No, Norman, you need to get it out. To tell me now." The smaller boy looked up at him, sniffled, and murmured, "OK," as they continued their walk toward the campus.

"Anyway, on the bank of this creek, tied to a limb of

a large tree, was a hanging rope of thick hemp. Someone tied it there years ago, and the older boys in the neighborhood would swing on it across the stream. There was a slight hill, an incline near the tree that enabled a running start, and holding on to the rope with both hands off; they'd go into the air across the stream. When reaching its highest point over the middle of the stream, gravity would bring them back to where they began the swing. In the spring, the kids would have to lift their legs up as they'd be so close to the water. In the summer, you could see the rocks in the river bed; the water would be so low, and you'd have to lift your feet high to avoid an encounter with the rocks. Norman slumped against a telephone pole, searching for his breath.

"Hal, I can't believe I'm telling all this. It's completely taboo at home. No one even acknowledges it happened."

"It's OK, Norman." He could change it to Norman at this emotional moment. "I'm listening. Please finish."

"Thanks, Hal. I'll get this out, and you will never hear me wail about it again." From somewhere beyond the dark houses, a dog barked.

"My mother had said more than once, 'Never take your sister down to the creek, and I don't want you taking that swing. I've seen boys doing it, and they're older and stronger than you.' What she didn't know was a couple of times that spring, an older boy took me on a swing with me holding on to him with one hand, the rope with the other, and it was great fun swinging the creek and back. I loved it."

They had reached a stand under the street light. Hal thought his roommate looked ghost pale. The moon had escaped its confinement from its black residence.

"It was an August afternoon; my Dad was at work, and Mom was at home in the house with a few women friends from her garden club. Carrie and I were playing in the backyard, and I decided to take her for a walk around the block to do something different. We were skipping, laughing, and calling each other baby names when I heard the sounds of excited voices and realized we were a block from the creek. I took her by the hand, and without really thinking about it, found myself leading her there."

As they passed under the next street light, Hal could see a tear slipping down Norman's cheek. Noticing Hal's glance, he brushed it away with the sleeve of his jacket.

"The temperature must have been ninety degrees, and the idea of taking a rest in the shade of the large tree and watching guys swing on the rope across the creek seemed a good thing to do. It was kind of like watching a movie, as I must have thought about it then. I was unwrapping a Milky Way candy bar to share with Carrie when Johnny Hagwood, a kid two grades ahead of me. Landed from his swing a few feet from where we sat. "Hey, kid. I'll give you a ride if you give me half that candy bar." I looked at Carrie, who seemed indifferent about the candy bar, so I agreed. Gave it to him, knowing the swing would take less than a minute and she'd be OK.

"'Hey, Eddie, come here,' Johnny called to a kid in his class. 'Norman, the Mormon, wants to take a turn. He's not a bad kid. I'll take him if you watch his sister.' He didn't mention I'd given him the candy bar.

Norman sniffed. "Of course, I wasn't a Mormon, but you know the way kids talk. Anyway, in a minute Johnny was next to me with the rope in hand. 'I'm ready to head home, but I'll give you one swing.' Before I realized it or thought about it, I was in the air, squeezing the rope with one hand and holding on to his pants belt with the other as we soared across the stream. As we reached the peak and began its return, I saw Carrie smiling and pointing at me. I felt so free and thought I could take this swing by myself. I was strong enough now. I was ten, nearly eleven. I could do it alone.

"'One more, Norman,' Eddie said.

"Thanks, Eddie, but I want to do one by myself." I suddenly felt older than my years. Johnny was still sitting next to Carrie and nodded approvingly.

Johnny said, "Let him do one alone. He can't drown if he falls off. Not enough water to fill a milk bottle."

"Eddie handed me the rope, and I pulled it a few steps up the incline, and with a hop, I launched into the air, and in that moment, I felt like Tarzan must feel on his vine. I let out a howl of delight as I reached the apex of the swing, followed by the pull of gravity that brought me back to the incline where I began.

Carrie ran up to me. 'That was great, brother,' she cried. 'I want to do it too. Take me, Norman. I'll hold on to you tight. I want to feel what it's like.'

"I said, 'Carrie, no, too dangerous. Time to go home.' My heart was still pounding when Johnny said, 'Yea, you aren't strong enough to hold her. I'll take her one swing. No more. Then I'm heading out too.'

"Carrie jumped into my arms. 'Please, Norman, let me have one swing. Johnny will take care of me.' Hal, I don't know what went through my mind. I was so stupid. I let her go. Johnny was strong and experienced. As soon as they were on the flight I knew it was a terrible mistake. I watched with increasing concern she might tell our mother, and I'd be somehow punished. Christ, the last worry I should have had. Anyway, as they began the return across the stream, it happened. She lost her grip; one hand slipped from his waist. She frantically tried to regain the hold, grabbing his belt, but she couldn't secure it. And then her other hand slid off the rope. I can see it now in slow motion. The sight never goes away. She fell from fifteen feet above the surface of the creek. I can see the terrified look on her face, like she was begging for me to rescue her as she crashed into a foot or two of water into a pile of rocks. Her body looked like a rag doll as it bounced off the stony surface. Her head collided with a rock."

The shadow of the campus buildings was now in sight. A car full of students passed by, windows down, and the Skyliners were singing "Since I Don't Have You." A Pittsburgh group, Hal thought.

Norman was entering the denouement stage of his story. "She suffered some kind of a fracture of her spine. She was hospitalized for two weeks. The doctors were in doubt regarding whether she would ever walk again without a brace. Still today, she walks with a limp. All because of me. I didn't leave my bed, couldn't eat for a couple of days. My parents thought I was having a breakdown. Not that that matters. I don't know if I'll ever be able to make it up to her, Hal. She is such a good girl, never blamed me in any way. Now she's a freshman in high school with a limp."

Norman grabbed Hal's arm for support. "It will be OK, Norman. You'll see."

What else could he say?

Chapter 17

Basketball practice began November 1st, two hours, four to six p.m., and Hal's life became busier. By the time he finished dinner with his teammates at the school's dining room, it would be past seven. From there, he would usually go to the library for an hour or two returning to his room tired and ready for bed.

As he became more acquainted with his teammates, he began spending more time off the court with them at meals, at the CSC, and occasionally at the Theta Mu house as a guest of two older players who were brothers there, sometimes accompanying them to a movie downtown.

The basketball team student manager, Charlie Altman, a sophomore who, after taping Hal's ankles before practice one day, said, "I have an aunt who has invited me to dinner Saturday. She lives about a dozen miles from here out in the middle of nowhere. Would you like to come along? Have a little home cooking?"

Hal learned what "in the middle of nowhere" meant. They drove seemingly an hour on a winding two-lane road that at times became a solo lane. Soon there were no houses visible. Hal opened the window, took a gulp of the cold mountain air, and gazed at a dazzling moonless sky with a million radiating stars, a sight never seen in the skies of Pittsburgh. Charlie slowed down and made a turn into a gravel road with only blackness ahead. They crawled past indistinct silhouettes of sleeping pines until the dim lights of the house appeared. Hal thought of the Hansel and Gretel fairy tale with the evil witch's hut deep in the forest. Charlie's aunt Rebecca was elderly but not a witch, nor was the house a gingerbread cottage. It was a one-story log cabin with a kitchen, a living room with a fireplace, and two bedrooms. He'd never been in a countrified house like this. He thought it was maybe like the house Abraham Lincoln lived in.

He and Charlie were in the kitchen watching his aunt fry some potatoes on the stove when she asked Charlie to get the milk. Hal didn't see a refrigerator and watched, astonished, as Charlie knelt down on the pine kitchen floor and pulled the latch of a hinged door on the surface. It opened to a view below of shelves with glass Mason jars, a skinned chicken or duck hanging from a wire rod, three or four label-less bottles of milk. Several large blocks of ice sat upon the dirt floor. It had never occurred to Hal that people lived without refrigerators. He now knew the meaning of "icebox."

*　　*　　*

Other relationships developed for Hal, mostly with his teammates, fellow freshmen Bill Hewitt, a 6'7 center from Sharon, PA, and point guard William "Willie"

Sutton from Bellaire, Ohio. One evening the three players attended a dinner at the home of the college's biggest athletic booster, Joe Newmaker, the owner of the only bookstore in town. Hal was seated next to Avril Ellis, owner of the retail store Clothes Closet, who said, "Hal, I'm hearing good things about you. Stop by next week. I have a sweater that'd would look good on you. Got your name on it."

On the Wednesday morning before Thanksgiving Norman was packing a suitcase full of soiled clothing and a couple of text books. Hal would remain in Lewisburg for the weekend because the team was playing in a two-day tournament at the state capital field house. He watched as Norman finished packing and gave him a warm handshake goodbye. "Say hello to your Mom and Dad. I know sister Carrie will be so happy to hear how popular her big brother has become at college. The only freshman writing for the school newspaper and your weekly column in the town paper."

After he left, Hal sat on his bed, savoring a few minutes of solitary time, reflecting upon the dizzying pace of recent events. As November followed October, he felt a change in his relationship with Norman. Fewer subjects of mutual interest materialized such that their conversations decreased in spontaneity, ardor, and frequency. As Hal pondered this change, he developed a theory: a strong relationship between two people built initially upon shared history and mutual interests inevitably weakens as the supply of new subject matter shrinks. Eventually, there would be nothing more of significance to know about the other person. Yes, the two could still find common ground discussing daily occurrences, but such quotidian and repetitive discourse is not the same as first-time revelations of unique experiences, personal interests, and beliefs. Repetition develops with its partner apathy in close pursuit. The vitality of the relationship withers.

Hal didn't mention this hypothesis to Norman, thinking it would likely hurt his feelings because he wasn't certain, there was evidence to support it. Hal labeled it "mining" since the more history and knowledge gained of the other person's mind is like coal extracted from the earth with the inevitability that each day there is less to mine. At some point, both the coal and the other person will be mined out. He wondered whether Norman felt it too.

Chapter 18

December passed quickly. The team played three games in a four-day excursion to the southern part of the state. Hal was the only freshman selected to the varsity travel squad. In one closely contested game with two starters having picked up four fouls, Coach Andrews inserted him into the lineup with ten minutes to play and the Cougars down two points. Hal responded with three baskets and a key steal sealing the team's comeback victory. The week before Christmas, Norman's first byline appeared in The Pharos, the student newspaper, with an article summarizing Calvin's three recent victories. The last paragraph breathlessly read, "Calvin's top freshman performer, six-four Hal Sparrow from Duquesne, PA, showed he is the real thing coming off the bench to spark the Cougar victory. With skill and maturity beyond his years, this freshman will make a solid contribution this season. And wait 'till next season!"

*   *   *

The presence and stature of both Hal Sparrow and Norman Emory were on the rise. So much so in the smaller boy's case, he acquired a nickname that year. He was in a meeting with the editor of *The Pharos,* who impressed with the quality and quantity of the article Norm wrote, exclaimed, "You are a real scribe. Nelson

Emory The Scribe." The tag stuck, and in a few months, he was known campus-wide as "Scribe." It took Hal some time, but he too soon began to call his roommate by his popular new nickname. Why call him Norman when others began calling him Scribe? Easier to say than Norman also. One less syllable.

*   *   *

Winter can paint a beautiful landscape in the center of the state. The slumbering hills and hollows engulfed in ground white; evergreens sotted with sagging snow tottering in the wind, and the deciduous trees, black scarecrows silhouetted against the gunmetal horizon. The view of the campus of Calvin College from the rooftop dome of the Lewisburg County Courthouse might have been a Norman Rockwell *Saturday Evening Post* winter cover of glorious winter in small-town America, "a picture print by Currier and Ives," as Johnny Mathis wistfully sang in his popular Christmas song that year, "Sleigh Ride." The Calvin scenes would have included the Colonial brick library building preening with multi-colored bulbs strung around its contour; the front doors of the dormitories draped in Holiday wreathes; the stone benches along campus pathways shouldering a foot of white, and the magical puffs of vapor accompanying each exhale, all fused to produce a rustic winter wonderland panorama, the likes of which

118

neither Hal nor Scribe, large city boys, had seen.

It was a snowy and windswept morning as Scribe was preparing to leave school for the Christmas holidays. Hal had to remain an extra couple of days for the last practices of the year. The two boys were in their room saying their goodbyes. Scribe had a hard cover book in hand and said, "Hal, you know I like the classics, Greek and Roman art and history. I'm giving you this book about the life of the great Roman Emperor Hadrian, who built the famous wall in England and ruled the Western world with a gentle hand. It's a great history of the Empire at its peak, but it's also a story of a relationship between the Emperor and his young assistant, Antinous. I thought you might like to read it over the holidays."

He handed Hal *Memoirs of Hadrian* by the Belgian writer Marguerite Yourcenar, the acclaimed definitive book on the life of the complex Roman ruler Hadrian.

When Hal, who spent the holidays in Sewickly, and Scribe returned to school in January, they had new experiences to share and discuss. That night in the room felt like their first days together in September. They chatted until late into the night, with Hal describing how good he felt as a guest at his headmaster's home in Sewickly with Mr. DePugh, his wife, and their two teenage sons and how they happy he'd been; they included him in all their holiday activities: a last minute

Christmas shopping tour in Pittsburgh's retail stores, a drive to the top of Mount Washington to see the mammoth Christmas tree with a thousand colored lights, the sumptuous Italian-style dinner at their cousin's home in Mount Lebanon, and the supernal church service with its 18th-century pipe organ and a forty-person choir caroling a dozen hymns. Hal said it was "like being with the family I never had." He added he had twice played basketball at a Pittsburgh YMCA with a number of college players and was pleased with the continued improvement in his game. Scribe had never heard him so expressive, so full of life, so happy.

It made Hal rethink his mining theory, but as the days passed and the euphoria of the holidays melted away like March snow, he became convinced it was more credible than not.

Scribe asked Hal if he had read the Hadrian book and, if so, what did he think. His roommate replied he liked it but was still formulating a more detailed analysis which he would share with him later. Hal's reluctance to discuss it was because he hadn't worked out in his mind whether Hadrian was of good character. Yes, the book made clear he was an emperor admired by his citizens and clearly an intellectual, versed in the arts and the science of the day, but Hal was troubled by Hadrian's relationship with the fifteen-year-old Antinous, which became sexual and ended with the boy's suicide. This relationship, integral to the story viewed through the perspective of contemporary 19 Century American morality, was what bothered Hal. Homosexuality was not a subject discussed at the CSC. He heard there were a couple of queers at Sewicley, but he never knowingly met one. Regardless it was not a subject he wanted to explore with Scribe, at least not at this merry time when the glow of holidays radiated in his heart.

Scribe reported on his cheery reunions with several high school classmates sharing first-time college experiences and what it was like to be away from home. He told of a happy time riding with his dad in his patrol car on the Pennsylvania Turnpike, looking out for speeders. His Mom told him he was too skinny and did her best to remedy that by going all out on a baking spree – cakes, pies, and, best of all, his favorite, Irish soda bread. He noticed, though this he didn't share with Hal, his mother at dinner when having to go to the kitchen to fetch a new course would take her empty wine glass and return with it filled. Scribe was so concerned about her drinking that he mentioned it to his father when they were alone.

"Norman, I am very concerned too, and as you know, I have spoken to her about it several times. She's in denial, I'm afraid. She has agreed to get some help and will visit a professional with experience in the problem right after the first of the year."

Scribe felt better and hoped counseling would rectify the problem.

He reported with a smile that his sister, Carrie, was in good spirits. Her limp was less noticeable, and she was scoring all A's in school. The accident was not mentioned, and Scribe decided, because of her cheerful frame of mind, to say nothing. He delighted in recounting the things he and Carrie did together: the hours one day in the town library, the two-holiday movies at the neighborhood theater, and the day a high school classmate took them for a ride through downtown Pittsburgh to see the stores' Christmas decorations. It was a happy reunion for the boys, one which would soon change for reasons unimaginable back on that carefree post-Christmas day of their freshmen year.

Chapter 19

The abounding mysteries of Calvin encountered in September with its new faces and voices, the uncommon buildings, the white steeple of the on-campus church, and its small-town homey ambiance were in the student's new year return to campus no longer so mysterious and imposing. The students halfway en route to upperclassmen status had acquired a modicum of confidence reflected upon increasingly blooming faces. Hal was doing well in his English courses, though not as well as his roommate. On the basketball floor, he was gaining stature daily, moving up to second man off the bench for the varsity. Scribe had secured his position as a freelance writer on the staff of the Lewisburg newspaper with a couple of accounts of student life. He was more the student, reading and writing at his desk late in the evenings after Hal, fatigued from a day in classes, time in the library between then and the vigors of basketball practice, had fallen asleep. Once Hal awakened to see Scribe whimpering, head in hands at the desk and wondered whether the cause was his mother's drinking, a recent setback his sister may have had, or a faltering relationship not revealed. Hal didn't want to disturb him, or maybe he didn't want to know what the boy's trouble was, and so he turned over in bed facing the wall and fell back into unconsciousness.

Then one late January practice Hal was racing down the side of the court on a fast break. He caught a pass twelve feet from the basket and flew high above the floor to finish a smashing dunk. At the peak of his leap, he collided with the backup center, who had emerged suddenly from his blind side. Knocked off the balance in the air, he tried unsuccessfully to break the impact of his fall with his hands, but his legs tangled, and he landed on the side of his right foot, a crushing blow. The pain was immediate. He could not move. His teammates rushed to his side, as did Coach Andrews, who whispered in his ear, "Don't move, Hal. I've got you. Help is on the way."

Scribe was in the dining room finishing dinner when two players, Todd Urish and Jerry Dawson, came rushing through the entrance. Scribe saw them, and his first thought was, where's Hal? They hurried to his table. "Scribe, we need to speak with you, now."

Todd and Jerry hustled him to a corner away from the tables. "It's Hal. He's had an accident. Went down hard on his ankle and had to be taken to the hospital."

"What?" Scribe said, visibly shaken. "An accident? The hospital? How bad is it? Has anyone heard anything from the hospital? What time did this happen? Where is the damn hospital? We have to go see him."

Jerry grabbed Scribe's arm and bent down to look

him in the eye. "There is nothing we can do now Scribe. This happened a half hour ago. I saw the ankle up close. I am afraid it's broken. He was taken on a stretcher to the hospital."

"Oh, God, no. Can't be." The guys at the dinner table were looking at them, sensing something serious had happened. Ted Wriston, who lived across the hall from Scribe and Hal hustled over. "What's the problem, guys?"

"Teddy, it's Hal. He's had an accident at practice. Broken bones in his foot." Scribe was rocking back and forth, losing his equilibrium. Teddy to Todd, "Oh no, not a broken ankle! Maybe it's only a sprain."

Jerry shook his head. "I'm afraid not. I was the guy who threw him the pass. I was right there. He was in the air, five feet from me, and I tried to reach him to cushion the fall, but I was too late. Guys, I played football in high school, and I have seen a lot of sprained ankles, and one break. Hal's fall was a bad one. I'm sure it's a break."

Teddy responded. "Let's call the hospital. Find out the facts. I've got a car. We'll go there, see him if we can." There was a pay phone in the dorm lobby, and Scribe hastened to it and asked the operator to call the hospital, identifying himself as Hal's roommate. He was still unable to get any information except, "Mr. Hal Sparrow is a patient in room 308. Please call later for more information."

Scribe, in his role as a correspondent for the town newspaper, had Coach Andrews' home number and called him. "Yes, Norman, it's not good. I just left the hospital. It's a broken ankle. He will recover, but I'm afraid Hal will miss the rest of the season."

At the hospital, the next morning Scribe found a very dispirited Hal Sparrow. He was lying in bed, his left leg elevated above his head. His foot and the lower half of his right leg was encased in a white plaster cast up to his knee. "Thanks for coming in, Norman. I'm trying to be positive, but it's a really bad break." He smiled feebly at the unintended pun, and his unconscious reversion to his roommate's given name. The use of his roommate's nickname, a convivial endearment, seemed to have lost its allure when Hal lost his future.

"Everything was too good to be true. Just when I felt on top of the world, this happened. Why me?"

Back on campus days later, Hal limped along, needing help the first two weeks to walk up the flight of stairs to his room. Scribe was with him at breakfast and dinner, at every possible moment. In the evening, back in the room, Scribe tried to cheer him up. "Your professors will all give you A's, the sympathy grade," and "You are now not only the most popular basketball player in school; you're the most popular kid in the school period, a legend as a frosh." And, more seriously, "Everybody admires your fortitude, your pluckiness. Everybody loves you, Hal. This will pass."

Hal tried to show pluckiness and fortitude but had a hard time mustering it. Sleeping with the cast was a fitful experience; he would awake numerous times throughout the night. The physical pain and discomfort was matched by his emotional agony.

Two weeks had passed since the accident. It was nearly ten at night. For the second or third consecutive day, the temperature was above forty degrees. The melting snow had created slushy walkways making it even more difficult for Hal to navigate between classes. The cast had been removed, but he was still hobbling around the disagreeably damp campus on crutches wondering whether he would ever dribble a ball again. Raindrops were bouncing off the windowsill. The cheerless weather added to the gloomy dimension Hal felt as he tossed in bed.

Scribe had not returned from an editorial meeting, and Hal was alone with his thoughts. The basketball team was in Kentucky for three games. How he missed his teammates, the practices, the games, and the small pleasures basketball yields, the squealing sound of sneakers on the hardwood floor, the familiar smell of the freshly washed socks and jocks, the grimacing looks from opponents as they line up for a jump ball, and the gratifying feeling of releasing the ball at the apex of his vertical leap, and watching it sail to the hoop.

Hal was a prisoner in his bed. He fought to focus on thoughts other than those of his season-ending injury and the pain in his ankle. He envisioned students at the CSC sitting in the booths sipping on Cokes, gossiping about campus romances, complaining about half-finished term papers, and feeding the jukebox dimes to hear Dion and the Belmonts sing "I'm The Wanderer" and Percy Faith's "Theme From A Summer Place."

For the first time, he wondered whether his father was dead.

He heard the footsteps advancing in the hall, the shaking umbrella outside the door. It opened with Scribe entering, switching on the reading lamp on the desk, and turning off the bright overhead light.

"How are you, my wounded hero? You're in everyone's thoughts. I stopped at the CSC and chatted up with the football guys. They asked me to tell you they want you on the football team next year. You are a two-sport star; we all know that." He smiled. "I told them they'd regret it. You'd get all the ink. How are you feeling tonight, roomie?"

"I feel like shit. I hobble around campus like the cripple I am. My foot and ankle still hurt, and all I think about is the missed season. And I hate this bed," whining as he struggled to turn on his side. "And Norman, thanks for asking. Do you think you could get me a Coke? I can't sleep anyway."

There was a Coke machine on the first floor, and Scribe hustled there, returning with two cans of the soft drink. "Let's listen to some easy music. We can talk. Maybe I can cheer you up. No pep talk, just real stuff, your future, and why I know it's so bright. I'll do everything I can to help you along the way if you need me."

Norman walked to his desk and took a seat. He fiddled with the dial of the clock radio until he found WWL, New Orleans, his favorite nighttime station, which played soft jazz until midnight. He adjusted the volume, enhancing the soothing sound of the music. He hoisted the desk chair, placed it on the side of Hal's bed, and took a seat.

"I noticed on your desk, Hal, you were reading Milton. I'm happy we got through Beowulf, Chaucer, and Bunyan's "Pilgrim's Progress" in the first semester. What do you think of Milton so far?"

"Norman, I'm trying to concentrate on my studies, but it's hard. I find "Paradise Lost" boring. I'm afraid it's lost me."

"Oh, come on, Hal, I'm writing my paper on it. Let

me tell you what I think. Milton is talking about Original Sin, which Eve committed when she bit the apple in the Garden of Eden. God forbade them to taste fruits there, and because she couldn't resist the temptation, we are destined to live a life of pain and suffering on earth. God punished Adam and Eve, who were embarrassed by their nakedness and forever inhibited and unhappy. Nice way to look at life, huh? But those were the times back in the 17th Century. "

Hal winced as he struggled to turn onto his back. Scribe pulled his shoulder in an effort to help him complete the turn from his side. "Thanks, Norman. I need help even turning. The whole thing stinks. I can't get riled up about Milton."

"Now, Hal, we're in the same class, and here's my thesis, and then I want to hear where you are on "Paradise Lost" and whether I can be of any help." Hal closed his eyes and nodded with minimum enthusiasm.

"Milton assumes God is great, and maybe he is but is he good? He purposefully tempted Adam and Eve into sin by showing them the delicious fruits of the Garden of Eden. It sounds like what my father says is entrapment, leading someone into a situation where they can steal and then arresting them. Would a good God do that? I say no. If God is not good, why should we believe in him? And why should we suffer for the sins of others?"

Hal hardly cared about Scribe's thesis. God or no God. Where was god when he needed him? The only good thing about today, he thought, was that it's the 20th Century, and nobody believed in Milton's bunk. What did I ever do to deserve to become a cripple, he thought for the five-hundredth time. It was not a question.

"Hey, that's great. Good for you. Scribe. But who cares about God when he doesn't give a damn about us? Milton, I don't give a damn about either. Maybe I'm not cut out to be an English major. I don't know what I'm cut out to be or do anymore."

Scribe leaned forward in the chair closer to Hal. "We don't know what God really wants us to do except not surrender to temptation. Well, that hasn't worked, has it? We're told He wants us to behave morally. Yet God doesn't seem to care if we kill each other. Christians killing American Indians. In the Thirty Year War in Europe, Catholics and Protestants murdered each other and their women and children. We believe we Christians are here to do good and to act with moral rectitude. Who could argue with the beliefs of loving your brother, being a good Samaritan, and obeying man's laws? But do we need God to live an ethical, moral life? Do we need to be threatened to burn in Hell in order to lead a life of honesty and goodwill? These were Milton's times when it was believed that sinners' fate was punishment forever in a place called hell. I'm writing Milton got it wrong. The God he writes about cannot be the real God if there is one. End of sermon, Hal, but that's my term paper theme on Milton."

Hal nodded vaguely. "Norman, that's great thinking. I'm impressed. But I have to tell you something." He paused in a wiggle seeking a modicum of comfort. "I'm thinking about quitting school."

Scribe's face lit up in shock, and he leaned in closer to Hal, his first word cut off by the boy in bed.

"Hold it until I finish, Norman." Hal grimaced as he struggled to prop his head up on the pillow. He had never before slept on his back, and now it was the only position he could endure.

"I spoke today on the phone with a guy I know in Pittsburgh. He thinks I could get a good job at U.S. Steel. The company has a basketball team of employees who play in the AAU, the Amateur Athletic Union, and they play other company teams throughout the area and the country, really. If you make the team, you get more money and work less in the mills. It's not ideal, but I'd be independent. Could get my own place to live and someday go back to college and get my degree. Maybe even take courses at night. The guy says the company would foot that bill, and I'd be soon in line for a junior management position, maybe in sales."

Scribe sunk back in his chair, absorbing this news."Hal, don't even think about it. You are far too intelligent not to get your education and degree now. Going to work, you'll find the money good enough that going back to school, even at night, will not be any fun. You'll never go back to school."

Scribe could barely contain his astonishment which had now morphed into anger. "Do you know what that means? Working in a company probably for life, not even knowing if you'll like it there? Never getting out of the shadows of Pittsburgh except to play some basketball games? And how many years will you be able and want to do this? Hal, come on now. Your life is here for four years, and you're not going to throw it away. You major in English, and get a job teaching and coaching basketball. That's what you've said you want to do. Everything is paid for here. You even have a summer job in Lewisburg if you want it." Scribe grabbed Hal's hand. "Think what Mr. DePugh would say. He came to your rescue. What about Coach Andrews? What about your friends here? What will they say and feel? What about me, Hal? I love you like family."

Hal closed his eyes. "If I could only make time fly. Get past this cripple stuff. You don't know what this is like, Norman. A minute is a week when you have no mobility and when you've lost the reason you are living. This is the end; one chapter is over. I need to begin a new one."

"Wait a minute, Hal. You say 'the end'! You're injured. Bad luck. You will recover soon. This is not the end. The cast is already off. You hardly need the crutches now. You will be working out by May, the doctor said. In three months, you won't even remember the pain, and you'll be playing ball in the Pittsburg summer league."

He took Hal's hand. "I feel strength. I feel comeback. I feel Hal Sparrow." Scribe was feeling like he never had before. He was seven feet tall. He was born to care, to dispense love.

"Yea, I don't know. I am so unhappy now, but it's just so fucking depressing being hurt and missing the rest of the season, the conference tournament."

"Hal, you need to stay at Calvin, to star, to become a man. I need to write about your exploits on the basketball court. I may become your biographer someday when you retire from your head coaching job at a big school, maybe even the pros. I can dream big for you. See you as a U.S. Senator--or whatever you choose to do. You have the brains and leadership qualities to be anything you want."

Hal had never known a person like Norman Emory,

who possessed both the maturity and wisdom to inspire in bad times. He could communicate; he could persuade. But Hal was not convinced.

"Hal, listen to me now. I have been thinking. You need a name, a special name, one that will be known to all here at Calvin. To every basketball fan in the state. You are a player, a major player. And, listen now, that is the name for you: Player. P, L, A, Y, E, R. You are PLAYER. You will be the star next season on the basketball court. And you told me you will audition for a role in the annual campus theatrical production. You will play leading roles, Hamlet, Caesar, or whoever the character may be. This will add to the meaning of your name, Player, known to all by this time next year. On the court, on the stage, and on campus, you will be Player in the hearts and minds of every Calvin student. And I will use that name in every article in the student weekly and the *Lewisburg Herald* when writing about Calvin basketball."

Scribe once again took his hand in his. "I have a story to tell you, Player. I believe in God or in some all-knowing being, some force that created our universe. But the emphasis on predetermination, the idea that the outcome of our life is completely out of our control, that we have no free will, is a terrible thing. It's wrong philosophy, wrong religion, and has no evidence.

135

Unfortunately, it's the Calvinist way of thinking that we are forever like children, incapable of shaping our lives. And only by suffering in life are we rewarded with a trip to heaven. Here, today in 1960, I think only the Pre-minnies believe in that doctrine.

"And another thing, in some countries, it's not a sin for a man to beat his wife; in others, it's all right to own slaves, and in others, homosexuality is a sin. I believe only killing, hurting, stealing, cheating, and interfering against the will of others are sins. We have chosen laws by men to punish sins and bring justice to those sinners have hurt. We don't need organized religion to govern our behavior and our lives.

"Hal, I gave you the Hadrian book to read because it's a story of love between two people. Two very different people, a man, and a boy. One is older, stronger, and more powerful. The other is young, intelligent beyond his years, and sensitive. They're very different in every way. But it was love that united them, that brought joy and happiness to each. Was there any 'sin' involved? Many, the large majority of Americans, would say there was sin. We are taught by the Christian Church, both Catholic and Protestant, that love with its pleasurable sex can only be enjoyed by married men and women. Love between those of the same gender is wrong, they say. God forbids it. And yet the Greeks and

Romans created great Empires, inspiring buildings and temples that stand today. They produced legendary thinkers, artists, architects, playwrights, and philosophers and they, both Romans and Greeks, thought a physical relationship between two men or between two women was love not sin. I do not believe that love like Hadrian and Antinous was a sin. The Greek and Roman gods did not object. Why would the Christian god object? Don't people have the right to love other people? Why should the opposite gender dictate?"

Scribe's face was close enough that Hal could feel his breath. Scribe's hand, which had been holding Hal's was now on his stomach, slowly inching in its journey to his crotch. This was not a wholly new feeling. Hal's own hand had taken this route to momentary pleasure. This was different. What should he say to Norman? What could he say? What laws of Nature, Man, and God should be my guides?

Scribe's hand was now inside the covers, inside the slit in the pajamas.

"I am here for you, with you, my Hadrian, the Player."

Hal felt the warm touch. Tasted Scribe's breath. He closed his eyes. His lips moved, but no words escaped. Where was his voice?

The voice in his head was Billie Holiday's "The Very

Thought of You." WWL's sign-off song.

Chapter 20

The Calvin experience begins upon arrival to the campus. It's a nervous time; peer faces are new, buildings are fortresses, and professors appear intimidating as the campus engulfs all within its womb.

Early winter brings snow, a yearning for home, serious exams, and term papers. Indoors boost friendships, potential intimacies, and focus on others. Embarking upon Christmas holidays, there are happy goodbyes at the dorms. The freshmen, when back home, will tell high school friends how great their college life is. Upon return to campus, they will exhibit a more studied strut and a confident insouciance.

Spring brings green and flowers, rainfall and rainbows, Bermuda shorts, sneakers, and sunglasses. Rides in somebody's car and finally finals.

The second and third years comfortably blend together in the minds of the now worldly-wise sophomores and juniors. The buildings are smaller, the food better, and the freshmen dumber. Exams and papers less stressful. New relationships blossom, and old ones wither or graduate.

The senior year brings the reality that their post-college future can no longer be ignored, and it passes in a week.

And so it was for our two boys. They went different ways after that long-ago incident in their room when Hal was bedridden. No longer would they room together. Their time as Mutt and Jeff had passed. Each mined out by the other and affected in unspoken ways by that incident that each kept secret.

Years two and three though still connected by a few English courses and their different roles in the basketball season, Hal "Player" Sparrow and "Norman "Scribe" Emory took separate paths, formed different cliques, found different rooms, Player off campus with a football player as roommate and Scribe in the dorm again but as a proctor focusing mostly on helping the freshman find their way. Player met Janet, and she dominated his social time. Scribe was still Scribe, everywhere seemingly all the time; thus, the subject of campus quips that there were Scribe doubles, more than one of the buzzing boy taking notes in his writing pad. His new job in the dorm produced needed additional financial assistance and punctuated the relative isolation the boys had from each other.

In their senior year, they were rarely seen together, and that was mostly in a group at the CSC or in after-game interviews. There was no overt animosity between the two. They were BMOCs, campus veterans who were aligned only by the sport and their chosen majors.

Perhaps a few of their senior classmates might remember they were once roommates, but college seniors find three years ago an eternity.

Chapter 21

At The Quarry, that busy day, Norman Emory was on Hal Sparrow's mind. As was his predisposition, Player kept his thoughts to himself. He had seen Scribe yesterday afternoon walking past the Science Building, alone, face down, with a satchel of books draped over his shoulder. Player was strolling along the walkway with Bethany and Bonnie in the opposite direction of the gothic sandstone girls' dorm. The girls were chattering about the movie they were headed to see, obviously pleased they had persuaded Hal to join them.

Ahead they saw Scribe wearing as so often, his gray Calvin sweatshirt with its washed-out orange representation of a golden cougar on his chest, shouldering a satchel of books strewn over his shoulder, approaching slow-stepped, uncharacteristic-ally solo. In her sing-song voice Bethany called, "Hail Scribe, the great Classicist. We're headed to the flick. It's *Breakfast at Tiffany's.* Wanna join us?"

Scribe plodded over to the group. "Hi, guys." His face wore an unhealthy pallor. He hadn't shaved, and the wisp of whiskers seemed to belong to a different face. "Thanks, but I'm really not up to it," he replied, mustering up a look of some-other-time.

"It's a happy movie. Cheer you up," said Bethany, who never needed a "cheer up."

Scribe nervously shifted his weight and looked up at Player. "Hal, could I speak to you a second, alone?" His use of Hal's name rather than his all-campus sobriquet signaled to the larger boy something of significance weighed on Norman. Player nodded to the girls and followed his one-time best friend to a spot a few yards off the sidewalk out of the girls' earshot.

"Hal, I need to speak with you about something important. Really important. Could we meet for a coffee.....in the morning? I don't want to intrude now, but I really need to talk, I need your advice. I am...."

"What is it, Norman?" Norman now too.

"Not now. It'll take a few minutes. Can we meet in the morning before you go to The Quarry?"

They had not met alone since the event, both presumably embarrassed it happened, and neither seemed to want to be the first to initiate the subject. Player's life had long ago improved after his recovery from the broken ankle, and his relationship with Norman could now be described as cordial.

"Yeah, sure. I'll see you at the CSC, OK?" Player equably replied.

"Hal, I'd very much like some privacy. How about the Hometown Market? Is 9 AM OK?.

Player woke early the next morning and turned on the bedside Zenith clock radio, the one he'd received from the town Rotary Club, "The College Athlete Sportsmanship" award, to hear today would be the warmest in April in years with the temperature flirting with ninety. He dressed in T-shirt, Bermudas, and sneakers and skipped out the door heading for town.

The pristine vitality of spring greeted him: the odor of the moist, earthworm-tilled soil; the budding green leaves on trees standing alert to the wind, the fresh fragrance of germinating shrubs, and the seductive aromatic hint of English Bluebell and Lilly of the Valley. Looking at the clock, Player realized he would likely be early for his meeting with Scribe and decided to take the more indirect route to town, bypassing the campus and walking the back streets of Lewisburg where families and real life lived. He strolled along Upsher Street past one-story houses where generations of coal miners and lumber workers had raised their families. He ambled past a number of aging, low-slung buildings that once homed freshly cut timber and then over to a new street where during the Fifties, a dozen split-level homes had been built in anticipation of Calvin hiring more professors. There he saw in the driveway of one a couple of elementary school boys shooting a basketball at a rim and backboard attached to the garage.

Player paused a moment, perhaps reminiscing of his boyhood days doing the same in the back alleys and playgrounds of his Pittsburgh neighborhood. One boy noticed him and pointed his way, shouting, "Look, it's Hal Sparrow." The other boy, picking up his dribble, said in an equally enthusiastic tone, "Player, sink one from where you are." He heaved a pass that took three bounces to reach Player, who easily fielded it with one hand and lofted a thirty-footer with a pinch of backspin that caused the ball, when making contact with the front of the iron rim to reduce its thrust just enough for it to gently bound upwards, off the middle of the wooden backboard and fall through the rim and frayed chords of the net. The boys danced in delight and sent a do-it-again-look. Player smiled and continued down the street.

Soon he was walking the footpath of the Birch River, now flushed with the last remains of the melting mountain snow and early spring rains. A half dozen town men hung over the side of the turn-of-the-century stone bridge; fishing lines stretched like rubber bands hoping for a morning catch of brook trout or spring bass. Across the river reigned the tracks of the Baltimore and Ohio Railroad upon which, a few decades ago, businessmen and vacationers rode in luxurious style to the great cities on the Atlantic. Moreover, before the end of the war, freight trains, the Great Iron Horses, pulling a hundred cars bursting with lumps of bituminous coal, rumbled north two, three times a day to the roaring steel factories that produced the twentieth-century products the American consumer craved. Today the frequency in which trains pass through Lewisburg has materially declined. Once a day was now a big event, and college students who were within eyeshot cheered merrily as the train rumbled by. Passenger trains had long ago ceased service in these parts, leaving grand classic train stations to sag into atrophy.

Player turned right off River Road, passing an abandoned dry goods warehouse that once distributed clothing and other household goods to towns throughout the state. Hal thought in the Twenties, and Thirties, Lewisburg, with twice its current population, must have been a beehive of commercial activity. Now it was an aging commerce-curtailed town dependent financially on the college. He wondered whether Pittsburgh someday would suffer the same fate. If the steel industry went the route of coal and lumber, migrating to lower-cost extraction and labor, would the city wither away? Whether or not Hal would be elsewhere in life.

A block later, he arrived at the town's business section. There was the owner-operated hardware store with a thousand products for sale; the pharmacy featuring a soda fountain and lunch counter and two hitching posts where once customers tied their horses; the all-American two-chair barber shop with its on-the-street red and blue candy-striped pole affirming its location; and the IGA store whose manager, like those in the six thousand other Independent Grocery Association stores nationwide, knew every customer's name.

Down a block was the quintessential first half of the century movie theater where yesterday he and the girls watched Audrey Hepburn as the split-personality Holly Golightly charming her befuddled pursuer. The theater was a structure to behold with its Greek marble exterior columns on granite walls, inside its walls, divided into large panels with borders and silken fabric and attractive sculpted figures gracing the 44-foot proscenium. Hal thought about something new in Pittsburgh called a shopping mall with multiple stores and a more functional three-screen movie theater and wondered how long this building would exist.

A storefront away stood the three-story limestone building that housed the all-purpose Woolworth department store. Above it, on the next two floors, were the rows of apartment windows with gray curtains impeding any view of the unknown occupants.

And there, off East Main, was the funeral home he and Scribe had passed so long ago after that first visit to the Old Town Tavern. Player stopped here, waiting to cross the street, and glanced to his right, where he saw his reflection in the window. It was odd unexpectantly seeing his full body image, yet it confirmed he was a physical being, a fixture in his world. He had taken a philosophy class and couldn't recall which great thinker talked about this. Was it Descartes, "I think therefore I am?" He thought I see too; therefore, I, of course, am. In a moment, he was standing before the signature edifice of the town, the stately, century-old County Courthouse building, a brick colonial structure with forty-feet-high marble columns and a Romanesque dome with a white-faced clock below the cupola, a deluxe building that could adorn any city in the country, he thought, as he stopped momentarily to absorb its magnificence. His time at Calvin had passed so quickly, and he wondered with mixed feelings whether he would return again after graduation. He wondered whether life ahead would speed by, a year like a month, a month like a day. The future was a foul shot away.

Nearing the Hometown Market restaurant where he would hear Scribe's problem, Player passed Lewisburg's only bookstore, its sign hanging above the sidewalk for all to see: "Newmaker's Books: New and Used." Joe Newmaker, its pock-faced owner, a middle-aged bachelor, was president of the Rotary and Calvin's basketball team's biggest booster. Joe never missed a home game in Player's four years. When the Cougars beat a worthy opponent in convincing fashion, Joe would appear in the locker room and shake hands with the standout players leaving in their palm a crisp one-dollar bill. Since he hadn't seen Calvin's most loyal fan since the season ended in March, he considered looking in the store to say hello to Joe, but his days on the court were finished, and Joe would now be turning his attention to those players returning next season.

*   *   *

When Hal arrived at Hometown Market, a restaurant featuring daily fresh baked pastries and squeezed orange juice, he saw Scribe in the same Calvin sweatshirt sitting in a booth back near the entrance to the kitchen. There was only one occupied table in the restaurant, and that; near the front door, where three local businessmen sat in amiable discussion. One looked up and acknowledged Hal with a "Nice season, Player. We'll miss you."

Hal took a seat in the booth across from Scribe, who reaching past his cup of untouched coffee, grabbed his hand in welcome.

"How you doing, Scribe? Haven't seen much of you these past few weeks."

The boy looked smaller than ever but a few pounds heavier since their freshman year. His right eyeglass lens was noticeably smudged, his hair drooping over both ears, and the football jersey he wore, a size too large and in need of a wash, added to his unkempt downbeat appearance. He had changed in other ways, Player now realized in the quiet privacy of his company here. There was a darkening shadow beneath both eyes, an incongruous supplement to his still adolescent face. Tiny creases crossed his forehead. It occurred to Player that the hurly-burly business of campus life, the passing seasons of both nature and sports, had dulled his ability to actually see or comprehend the physical changes in the people with whom he had spent four years at Calvin, how the mind can fail to register what the eye beholds. Or does the mind, distracted with other thoughts, ignore or conceal visible reality?

The waitress arrived at the table, and Norman spoke up, "Anything for breakfast, Player, or Hal Sparrow? It's on me. Thanks for coming."

Hal ordered scrambled eggs, toast, and orange juice. Norman followed with the same and a refill of his coffee.

"Jesus, Hal, where did our years go?" The use of his given name indicated the serious nature of the meeting.

"Yes, it seems like yesterday," Hal responded languidly. He would address Scribe as Norman and disregard the once kinship and familiarity that was stamped out by the incident, as Hal had learned to think of that moment in their dorm room four years ago. Words mattered, and using the word "incident" ameliorated the shame and confusion he still felt.

"How have you been, Hal?" Norman began. "Seems like our nicknames will not be a part of us much longer."

There was a lull. Norman, uncharacteristically seemed to hesitate, thinking perhaps how to start with the troubles he brought with him.

"That's true. College will soon be behind us."

He waited for Norman's response, but the boy seemed obsessed with his coffee cup, staring it down and fiddling with it like it was an old forgotten toy of some sort, a spinning top at rest, perhaps.

"What's up, Norman? You wanted to see me, and here I am."

There was an absence of history that hung over the two like a motionless cloud on a windless day. The words needed to express the end of an era, to wave goodbye to friendships, and to leave the physical environment are as difficult to retrieve as fireflies in the night, easy to see when blinking but difficult to catch.

"On another subject, Player, damn it, I'm sticking with Player a little longer," Norman breathed audibly. "All this hazing stuff, you on the committee to decide Theta's fate. Finals; coming up in a month or so. It's been a while since we've talked, and I appreciate your meeting me today. You decided yet what you are going to do after graduation? Last time we talked, you were thinking about either coaching or going into some corporate management-training program. You'd be so good teaching and coaching kids."

His sad eyes suggested he was wondering whether he would ever see Hal Sparrow again after graduation. New lives begin, and people go live and die in different ways and places. He thought Hal would be like that, like those graduates who seldom, if ever, return to their college. His head slid down into his hands, elbows on the table as he peered into his coffee cup for a long moment.

Norman Emory, who had taken a minor in Psychology and likely ranked in the top ten of all students in reading the most books in four years, knew that disappointments and setbacks in life can arrive with a sudden vengeance. He knew young people usually needed more time to bounce back from misfortune. He had counseled others in distress at Calvin. It would pass, time heals, and you'll forget about it before the next semester arrives was his message, and he was usually right. The best example of this was sitting across the table from him now. Hal may have now been sitting in the cafeteria of US Steel or on the road with fellow basketball employees to play a semi-pro team in Oshkosh.

However, the very advice Norman had given others didn't apply to him now. Not relevant when the pained one was himself. Maybe he had never believed what he was proselytizing to others. Maybe he lacked the intellectual and moral substance that his reputation was based upon. Maybe, he, with the heralded nickname, Scribe, given out of respect by his boss at the town newspaper paper and readily adopted by the school body, was a lie. Maybe he had conned himself and everyone else.

Hal was about to ignore Norman's question, sensing the boy was seeking companionship and affiliation but something within, a modicum of empathy arose to his consciousness, and his words actually followed.

Hal produced a genuine smile, the one "Norman, thanks for asking about me. I'll give you the short version."

"Not sure what to do. I have that corporate offer, but the job is in New York, and I don't know if I'm ready for that. As far as teaching and coaching high school, I've applied to several high schools in the state, but only a few assistant positions are available, and none include teaching English. So I am waiting a little longer to see if any such openings occur. Meanwhile, as you likely know, Janet's been teaching in Baldwin, living at home with her parents. Her father owns two radio stations in Pittsburgh and wants me to work with him, learn about the business, and help him make it grow. I'm flattered, of course, but not so sure it's a good idea. But I'm also feeling a little pressure to take the big step. Janet wants to start a family soon."

Norman smiled for the first time today, a parade of pink returning to his cheeks. He spoke with the old energy in his voice.

"That's great news, Hal. You deserve the best, and I know you will make the right choice. Janet is a terrific girl, more good for you."

Norman took the first bite of his now cold scrambled eggs and downed what remained of his coffee. He attentively pushed the plate and cup slowly to the far side of the table and erected himself in the seat. His eyes met Hal's directly, held for an uncertain moment, and then faded downward into emptiness.

Hal said, "Norman, you said you needed to speak with me. I'm here."

"OK. I'm sorry," he hesitated like an actor who momentarily forgot his opening lines. "I got bad news from my mother two days ago. Something happened in my Dad's department at work. She said it had to do with internal politics. Then she says he was forced to resign, to quit his job. Those were her words, but when I asked what that meant, she said she wasn't sure. I called the next day, yesterday, twice in the morning and afternoon. She said he hadn't been out of his room since

Wednesday night, when he arrived home much later than usual. I asked to speak with him, but she refused, saying he wasn't ready to talk about it. What happened, I asked, but she would only say, "I'm not sure. I'll call you back as soon as I know more.'''

Scribe lowered his face into his hands.

Hal said, "I am sorry but doesn't your Dad have seniority? Isn't there a police union? Does he have a lawyer?"

"Shit, Player, I don't know any more than I just told you. Oh, God, we, my Mom and sister, are so upset...." He managed to look up. His eyes were welling. He slumped back in his seat. He looked like an abandoned washcloth.

Hal paused, thinking about this. "Have you called again today?"

Norman wearily choked, fighting away the big bang of tears he felt coming.

"No, that's the other thing. We usually talk every other week on Friday around dinnertime. I called again last evening, and this time he came to the phone. He said, "Son, it will be all right. I can't get into specifics right now. Don't you worry? Get that degree, and when you get home, we can talk. I'll know more then. Love you, son.'"

"What do you think 'internal politics' means?"

Norman talked past this. "Mom's health has deteriorated over the last year or so, and I'm petrified this thing with my father will cause a complete breakdown. Internal politics? I have no idea, except he must have had a problem with his boss. I never met that guy, but I think he was new to the force."

He stopped to take a sip of what would likely be cold coffee. "I can't believe it had to do anything with doing with job. He has had many citations from Harrisburg." He paused and, with difficulty, continued, "Maybe he's involved in a scandal of some sort; I don't know. I told her I would come home today, but with exams coming up, she said she would hear nothing of it. 'Stay, stay,' she said, 'you will be home soon enough.'"

Norman showed a look of helplessness that he had not revealed on campus, ever.

Hal, sensing there was more, remained silent.

"And here is the other thing." Norman glanced upwards at the ceiling as if heaven was observing. He noticed for the first time it consisted of white tin squares, and there was a lone fly circling around it, thinking perhaps it was an escape window.

"Hal, my parents have paid a substantial amount of my college expenses. My student aid covered about half the cost, but over four years, the difference adds up to a lot of money, and that has been a sacrifice. We don't have much money and if my father's firing is because he got involved in something illegal, pray to God no, he might not be employable. Maybe he'd even lose his pension. I doubt my mother, with her health problems, could find a decent job. There may be unknown medical costs to care for her…"

"But hold on, Norman, you don't know the facts yet. Don't know why they fired him if they did. And I would think he will find another job; he is not that old…"

"Hey, thanks, Hal, but that's all he knows, being a state policeman, patrolling the highways. What else could he do?"

A lonely tear streamed slowly down his face, missing his nose. Hal handed his unused napkin across the table.

"And here's another problem…Oh, shit, you don't need to hear this stuff, Hal…"

"Please, Norman, talk to me. That's why I'm here." It was Hal's emotion-free voice, the one he employed when communicating to teammates on the floor or when asking a professor a question.

His empathy, however was being strained. Norman was so emotionally upset he could not deconstruct each element of the problem. Maybe his Dad was innocent. Maybe his job loss was a temporary suspension. His mother was maybe not the best information source. Maybe Norm should go home today and deal with the situation.

The usual witty and incisive-thinking Norman Emory, known by all for his ability to communicate orally and in writing with Aristotelian logic, seemed to melt into the booth, incapable of clear-eyed thinking.

"My sister, Carrie, is a junior in high school, you know, and she is smarter than me and has always wanted to go college. I don't know how she can now that my dad has no job." He stopped abruptly, thought uncompleted, fighting the train wreck that had crippled his mien and threatened his very being.

"Norman, pluck up." That's the message his coach at Sewickly voiced when a player showed on-court despondency or lack of effort. "I'm sorry, but things are never as bad as they seem at first." Maybe Hal was thinking of his state of mind when he broke his ankle, provoking unwanted and immediately dismissed thoughts about the incident; he looked away from Norman for relief.

"Why not leave today, now? Go home. You will feel better. You could hitch a ride and probably be there by dinner time."

Scribe shook his head. "Then I'd have to tell them my bad news. I'm not ready for that today."

"What do you mean; your bad news?"

"Aw, fuck, Hal. I hate myself for dumping all this on

you too, but you're my first and oldest friend on campus, and who else can I really talk to?"

Hal thought quite a few students, Norman's campus experience having more contact with more people than his.

A well-dressed middle-aged couple with the look of visiting parents took a seat behind them in the next booth. Hal had the view and saw they were looking their way while Norman was losing the fight to control his emotions.

"Come on, let's get out of here, Norman. We can take a walk down by the river. No one will be around, and the fresh air will help." He put two one-dollar bills on the table and led the boy out the door down the empty side street to the path along Birch River.

Sniffling, Norman said, "Thanks, Player, if you don't mind me calling you that one more time. Time passes so damn fast and where it leads, who knows. I know I have to stop this self-pity and pluck up," this with the disappearance of the trepidation his face wore. " But I have never been so upset, so discouraged."

"You mentioned something else. 'My bad news.' What is it?"

The sun was now radiating above the hilltops, the sky robin egg blue. Ahead the river flowed smoothly, two visual signs that the universe worked as usual and that it would exist long after the quotidian contentedness and trivial woes inherent in those who strolled past it.

The weather forecast promised to be reliable this day.

"I didn't want to mention this burden to you anymore, but in light of what has happened to my father... but this I fear, I know is even worse....". He was interrupted by a couple of students passing by on their bicycles, waving their good mornings.

"Here is the end, my end. I was really certain that I would get that job." He paused, steadying himself against the trunk of an elm tree with limbs hanging over the river, to inhale a deep breath of air and wipe his eyes with the restaurant napkin he had commandeered.

"Didn't tell anyone about it because I was afraid telling someone might jinx it, but in March, I applied for an apprentice job with the *Pittsburgh Press*. They had two openings for college journalists graduates. I prepared a booklet with the best of my articles from here, both in the Pharos and the local paper. I wrote a news story about the Pennsylvania State legislature contemplating a hike in the sales tax. I interviewed at the *Press* with three different managers and was confident I had the job. Yesterday I got the letter. 'You are an accomplished writer and will make a good reporter, blah, blah, but we're sorry'....."

He stopped; his body stood still, arching backwards

as if struck by an arrow.

Hal stopped too, feeling the pain of the boy's loss of the job, a failure to attain a major early life goal. He spoke in a tone never called upon at Calvin, its timbre laced with true emotion, the opposite of his voicelessness at the horrible accident in the beer distributor's plant.

"Oh man, Norman, I'm so sorry…."

"Hal, I depended on getting that job and planned to surprise my parents with the news and tell them I would help pay my sister's college expenses. Carrie's been accepted to Pitt, and it's fucking expensive. Now I've no job. I'm a loser, and now she is too because of me." He kicked an empty cigarette package that littered the path.

They walked another twenty yards in silence. "Thanks for listening, Hal. I'm going back to the room. I can't go home today. No one would even pick me up if I hitched. I'm such a loser."

Hal grabbed his arm. "Norman, stop feeling sorry for yourself. First of all, with your academic record and award-winning journalism here, you will definitely get a good newspaper job somewhere. How many newspapers have you sent your resume to?"

Scribe choked on his response. "Not many." Hal stopped him looking down into his eyes.

"Well, one other. The *Gazette,* but they're not hiring

graduates this year. But no, I've really thought this job was in the bag." Head hung lower, I could get a job teaching, maybe, but I love reporting; journalism. It's all I ever wanted to do."

Hal thought it was not unlike Norman to assume he had something he didn't. He was always so self-assured that what he believed to be true was, without a doubt ,true, and what he believed would happen would.

"Tell you what. If you don't want to go home, don't spend the day sitting in your room. This is spring, and nature has its way of cheering us up. I have a ride out to The Quarry at noon with Joey. You come along. There will be a lot of people there, and you can forget your troubles for a moment. That is if you really don't want to go home today."

Norman nodded, "Thanks, Hal. Maybe I'll see you out there."

"Be good for you, and meanwhile, when you are thinking about something else, the problems you think are insurmountable usually go away. Remember when I thought my life was over four years ago? You told me I was wrong, and you were right. Now I'm telling you you are wrong. OK, now?"

He surprised himself by alluding to the incident and waved Norman goodbye.

Chapter 22

Some of those in Player's group above the fabricated beach and black water had wandered off and joined others. Nonetheless, several male and female students now congregated around him. As Tommy Teller was chatting about his job offer from a Pittsburgh accounting firm, Player thought again of Scribe's plight. He noticed that Nelson was no longer with the group. He felt a sudden instinctive concern and looked around to see where the boy had gone.

Because it was the first perfect weather day of the year, the quarry was particularly crowded. Calvin kids, who usually remained on campus for whatever reason, were now sprouting like dandelions in an unkempt yard. Player inspected the assemblages of mingling students, scanned the beach, and looked beyond the parking lot. The increase in milling students made spotting individuals more difficult.

He didn't see Scribe.

On the other side of the water was the towering slate rock boulder, the looming natural monument notoriously known as the site for The Dive. The black water below the boulder sent our sun sparkles. Player noticed heads turning in that direction and looked up to see Scribe, back bent low, hand after hand, clawing up the craggy rock like a pack mule scaling a mountain. What the hell was the Scribe doing there?

Only three times had Hal seen someone other than Forrest and Joey K climb to the top of the boulder. Neither attempted "The Dive," as it was referred to. The student legend was a few years ago, one guy, a dispirited athlete who had been told his services would not be needed next season, reached the top, looked long and hard at the flight to the water below, and then retreated back down. Another, a bumptious kid from Connecticut, marking time at his third college in as many years, bragged that taking The Dive was a "walk in the park." Supposedly motivated by a large wager, he took the leap giving the middle finger to his awe-stricken Calvin mates before crashing into the water, breaking both legs. The third guy, who was an overweight and overwrought wastrel known for his peerless patronage of the two town's roadhouses, reached the boulder's precipice, pulled from his pants pocket two green banknotes, and dangling each bill in different hands he, yelled out, "In God We Trust." Then launched himself feet first, striking the water with such impact its shower dampened those sitting on the beach. After an agonizingly long spell beneath the frigid water, he surfaced breathless and ghostlike and was rushed in a frat brother's car to the town hospital.

Player when known as Hal, once during his freshman

year, was offered twenty bucks to take The Dive and without hesitation refused. No one thought he was a chicken.

*   *   *

Player, who, like many others, had by now noticed the skinny BMOC ascending the boulder, was shocked. Stunned, a sight he could have never imagined. Norman Emory was the last student who should be making the climb, but in Hal's mind, even if Norman could make the sixty-foot climb up the thirty-five-degree angled boulder, he would dare not jump. He realized how upset Norman was, but no amount of anguish should prompt anyone except a well-conditioned athlete to take The Dive, particularly not a fragile one-hundred-and-thirty-pounder.

Perhaps Scribe only wanted to attempt to scale the boulder to show everyone he was more than a campus intellectual buzzing like a bee around the campus, more than a guy who wrote about the physical feats of others but was deprived of any athleticism himself.

Maybe this bizarre climb was a momentary escape from the troubles he had spilled upon Hal this morning. Even though Norman was in significant distress, he had seemed in better spirits when they parted, but he was here at The Quarry, as Hal had advocated. Only minutes ago, he had vigorously participated in the group's

165

discussion of the Theta Mu situation, showing a determined point of view on the major ongoing issue affecting all his fellow students.

Hal thought he had convinced the boy that there was insufficient information about his father's situation. And why couldn't his dad get another job, a trained state policeman must have skills some local police departments and maybe some companies could use. Norman would surely find a good job at a newspaper somewhere, which would help offset the financial need his sister had to attend Pitt, and if she was as smart as Norman said, she would likely get financial assistance. That solved that problem, Hal told Norman. He had made these points, hadn't he? But maybe not as forcefully as he could or should have.

But what the hell was Norman doing trying to scale the bolder, having the full attention now of half the student body? It was a bold, totally ignorant, desperate move. But Hal believed when Norman reached the peak, if he did, he would quickly begin retreating back down, and if he needed help descending, he and others would be there to help bring him safely down to earth.

*   *   *

There was, during this shinny-up exhibition, the thumping rise of a growing minority of multiple voices, mixed messages voices, animalistic and tendentious, here and there. *Show us your stuff, Scribe! Come back now; enough. Enough! You gottcha big balls, little man! Be careful, Scribe! Take the Dive. You can do it,"* rang out another chorus.

Scribe was out of his mind, but there was no hesitation, no sign of indecision. He was decidedly and carefully, step by step, conquering the boulder, headed to its top plateau. Not all the shouts and screeches were distinctly discernible, sucked into the vortex of greater voices, into black holes of student cries. Some nearby huddled students, Hal noticed, were staring expressionless in awe as if finding themselves in a different classroom with a different professor and different classmates, not believing what their eyes told them was a reality. Others, not yet joining the crowd in its fearsome focus, nervously confused by what they saw, could voice only "oohs' and "ahhs." That aside, there was a growing interest, fascination it was, in the spectacle of the body belonging to Scribe ascending the boulder, a performance never seen by the majority.

Tommy Teller leaned over and said to Player. "What the hell is Scribe up to? Has he lost his marbles?"

Hal stared at the climbing figure of his one-time best friend. If this insanity was triggered by a couple of beers, the effects would be wearing off as Norman was expending considerable energy clawing his way up the towering boulder. This was Tiny Tim a couple hours ago in tears, despairing of his bucket of troubles. Now he was Super Boy showing the audience he was more than a scribe writing the stories of others. He was now in the story; he was the story, a one-man athletic performance of Olympic magnitude. That he was suddenly the boldest kid in school?

Hal didn't get it and turned to Tommy.

"Yea, I can't believe it either. Maybe he wants us to remember him as something more than just the best sportswriter we've ever known. He'll turn around any second now and work his way back down. Join me in going over and helping him down."

At this moment in the spectacle Player, Tommy, and their group were joined by Joey Cappollo, the school's best athlete and possibly its worst student. All the jocks knew Joey could have played Division One ball, except his high school grades and test scores were rock bottom. At the CSC, where Joey could be found six hours a day, he often struggled in social conversation. Part of that was because he was raised in an overcrowded Catholic orphanage where children were to be seen, not heard. Part was because his audience imagined he was the school fool, a Shakespearian fool, funny and loved by all. Joey enjoyed the habit of voicing loud and shocking pronouncements like "You've got sneaker breath, ha, ha." Or, "Your armpits are pissing sweat, ha, ha."

"Hey, Player, what the fuck is Scribe up to?" The sound of Joey's voice rose above the low din of nearby groups. Most Calvin socializers in the audience had become increasingly quiet, spellbound, wondering what would happen next.

"I don't know what he is trying to prove, Joey. Christ, he's within feet at the top. Come on, Scribe, come on down," Player wailed with increasing volume.

A junior coed, Lois Fuller, called "Tuesday" because of her remarkable resemblance to actress Tuesday Weld, was standing next to Tommy Teller. Known for voicing strong and intelligent opinions on any subject, she chimed in.

"He's just showing off, guys. Only wants to have some fun today. Show us his game instead of writing about someone else's. Let's see what he does when he is at the top; maybe he will read his last column in the Pharos."

Hal looked at Tuesday, his humor, if any, he'd left this morning at the Hometown Market.

"I doubt that," he replied. "I thought he would give up before he got to the top. But he's too smart to try The Dive." Hal figured he was the only person here who knew the state of his classmate's mind. He also believed Norman was reliving some fantasy that he could be the lead name in the headlines of a story of conquering the legendary boulder at the Quarry. This climb was the expression of his long-yearned-for desire to be someone he wasn't, at least for a moment. His troubled mind was the driver for this today.

"Sure, he's too smart, Player, and he's a scaredy-cat too. He's putting on a show, and I say let's sit back and watch the ending." Tuesday's smile could persuade a county judge to dismiss all charges against her.

Joey, exchanging looks with both Player and Tuesday, began and finished with, "Ha, ha, ha. Scribe's got a screw loose. He might slip and break his ass. He might think he can fly, ha ha, reading all those funny books he reads in those English classes you guys take. You know, Player?"

Gazing from his vantage point on the grassy knoll Hal watched the growing mass of Calvin students matching in number that of a homecoming football game, scrambling for positions to enjoy the spectacle Scribe was successfully creating. Voices of various tones, pitches, and volumes reverberated throughout the quarry locale, a crazed chorus like a concert crowd urging Elvis Presley to the stage.

Hal felt a sudden alarm that the fervor of the crowd could stir Norman's excitement, boost his recklessness and contribute to his fall from the boulder. Worse, he thought, though dismissing such notion as unrealistic pessimism, the increased crowd cacophony could spur Norman, already feeding off the arousal of his audience, to do the unthinkable. To take The Dive.

As Norman neared the top of the boulder, a stunned Hal Sparrow could hardly believe his eyes. It took him a long moment to accept what he was hearing and longer to believe what he was seeing. The boy had reached the top of the boulder and now stood on its flat plateau fifty feet above the black water of the quarry. Was he trying to send a message that there is no obstacle we humans, with desire and effort, cannot overcome? Is he trying to send a wordless message, a metaphor for something? Man's triumph over nature or over physics? Might it indicate a manifestation, consciously or unconsciously, of long-concealed narcissism, the product of the tangled formative forces of Scribe's nature and nurture?

Was Scribe now finished, perched on the peak of the boulder? Surely he was. He'd flag a here-I-am gesture of some kind, heroically bow to the sure coming standing ovation, then pivot about-face and begin his slippery descent back to earth. That's where Hal would join the few Kent Ayers-led Theta Mu's who were already at the boulder base preparing to make safe Scribe's downward crawl.

He was now standing on the plane of the boulder

about twenty feet from the edge. He was swaying slightly, a sign, Hal thought; the climb had shortened his breath and used energy needed to maintain firm footing. He took a few short steps forward; looked out and down at the crowd.

"My God," a voice nearby yelled above the crowd chorus, "what's he doing now?"

What he was doing now was clear for everyone to see. He was struggling to remove his Calvin sweatshirt. For a moment, his face was out of sight; his head stuck under the front side of the jersey, one arm flailing like a wounded duck, the other fighting for release from his body. In the time it took to skip from the science building to the library, he succeeded in the removal. He two-handed massaged until it acquired the approximate shape of a football. He took two more steps towards infinity and held the jersey one-handed, high above his head like a wide receiver might do with a football after a spectacular touchdown catch to give the fans an extra jolt.

"Go for The Dive, Scribe," one guy, a red-headed footballer standing beer can in hand not far from Hal, howled when the crowd noise increased as Norman took another step toward the boulder's edge. Then, with what some would claim later was a titanic smile of triumph, he retreated five yards with jersey ball in right hand, extended his throwing arm back behind his shoulder like Bobby Lane, his Steeler QB idol, and with a hop forward threw a fifteen-yard toss that narrowly cleared the rim of the boulder, momentarily levitating upwards counteracting the force of gravity with an assist from a burst of Allegheny wind, followed by its unraveling, a long-sleeve Calvin jersey again, dizzily drifting like a homemade kite into the black waters of the quarry.

A huge crowd roared, some standing ovations, a few laced with congratulatory profanities, words only whispered on campus. Arms stretched in glorious tribute, hands eagerly meeting in slapping spank. Scribe had electrified the audience, his performance uniting in a frenzy the four classes of the student body, though Hal saw only a handful of pre-minnies.

Joey's voice, "Think you should call him down, Player. Goddamn, kid's a disaster waiting to happen. Poop his pants next." There was no ha, ha, ha.

Near the bottom of the boulder, several Theta Mu's had gathered. One, Kent Ayers, had begun climbing the rock. Others were scrambling up behind him. If needed, the Greeks were ready for the rescue.

Scribe, standing near the edge, showed the raised two-handed pose of the boxer who had KO'd his opponent. He glanced skyward into the blue in appreciation of the help from the heavens, or was it a homeward-bound look?

Hal wondered what Norman's father, pictured laden with medals of valor and service in the framed photograph in his vest Norman kept on his bedside table, would think. Two Emory's in precarious conditions? He thought how the boy's mother might be reacting to the bad news back in McKeesport, alcohol her salve? His sister, unaware if she was, that Norman's lack of post-graduation job yet would likely make her attendance at Pitt a more challenging reality.

The crowd voices lowered again, apparently waiting for Scribe's next move, which was to wave paternalistically to the crowd, to his fans below. He gave them the Joe Palooka muscle man pose, shirtless, flexed biceps, stern visage, a face of granite. He changed stance extending his arms parallel to the rock surface, his head drooping sideways. Jesus, nailed to the cross.

My God, thought Player, Scribe has lost his mind. What is he trying to say, to be?

Ayers, followed by two other Mu's was nearly at the top of the boulder. They would bring Norman Emory down to safety. Where was he, Hal Sparrow, the widely acclaimed Player, a leader on the court. Where was he now at The Quarry? A thinker only distanced from the action?

A moment passed, breathlessly for most, as Scribe

took the last step to the end of the boulder and gazed below – a look of willful contentment on his small face. Player thought surely this was his final gesture before scaling back down the boulder. But he was less sure and could no longer sit and watch. He leaped to his feet and began running, looking for a path between the crowd, to the boulder.

Norman Emory, a most accomplished senior student at Calvin College from a small city in Western Pennsylvania, lifted his arms upwards like Moses in the desert, reaching for God when surrounded by the Amalekites army. The aroused students responded Roman Colosseum style with full-throated cheers and jeers. There came the mad voices of those whooping encouragement to Scribe to take The Dive. Those in opposition, their voices drowned out by the mad clamor of those demanding more excitement, demanding The Dive.

As Hal found traction through the throbbing crowd, he heard the screams of "Go for it. Take the Dive, Scribe. You're the man."

Hal was moving winged-feet Mercury speed-bumping non-moving students out of his way. Still, he was half a football field away from the boulder; from the boy. The crowd noise made it unlikely he would hear Hal's shouts."Norman it's me. I'll be with you in a moment. Back away, Norman." Let him know it's me, still his friend through it all. All this his mind heard, his voice screamed, but Norman had not looked his way.

Silhouetted against the cloudless sky, Scribe waved appealingly to the crowd, a gesture seeking quiet. The circus in his mind had never been so real. His mouth opened, and his lips moved; despite the crowd quieting, his words could not be heard. At that instant, a large crow, coal black as the Devil was red, appeared from behind the boulder, cackling, caw, caw, caw, gliding over Scribe's head. He gave it a nod and peeled off his Bermuda shorts, clad now only in underpants and sneakers.

A voice screamed out above the restrained voices of the crowd banter. It was Joey C on his feet, jumping, screaming, "Don't do it, Scribe. Stop. Now! Goddammit."

Scribe seemed to hear Joey's plea, looking down upon him. Scribe took one, two, three steps back – back to safety, sanity. He had heard Joey's voice, his plea. Player heard it, too.

"Get your ass down here, now, Scribe," Joey roared. No. Ha, ha, ha's. It was indeed Joey K's voice, so often missing or confusing that now rang out like overhead thunder demanding Scribe not take The Dive.

Ayers was on the surface of the boulder, a dozen feet

from Scribe speaking to the boy, words inaudible to the throngs on the ground. Scribe, now naked except for his underpants and sneakers, had re-stepped to the precipice of the boulder, and, like an Olympic diver on the end of the board, he took a deep, exaggerated inhale of the Appalachian air. Watch me now was his expression.

Player howled. Player roared. Player wailed. "Scribe, Norm. Norman Emory. It's me, your roommate! Milton! Byron. Shakespeare. Stop! Come down here! Now. This second."

Crowd silence. Two BMOC, once frosh roommates, Mutt and Jeff, now commanded the attention of all at The Quarry.

The spring breeze that tickled the hollows departed, sucked out by the human drama. Only the trailing sound of the crow's caw interrupted the silence throughout the Quarry.

Scribe hesitated, looking down at the crowd, and then again took the three steps back from the boulder's edge. Ayers was beckoning him; hands outstretched, speaking it seemed calm.

Player was back at the foot of the bolder. "No, no, Norman, No. We love you! I'm Hal Sparrow. I love you! Come down!" Player screamed. Player's voice in full throttle beg. Scribe may have heard Hal's voice through those who talked about it later. Player began his ascent, a monkey-like climb dash to the top. To save the boy he knew he would ever miss.

Scribe made a motion with his hands and arms, like he was shooting a free throw, a perfect follow-through. He looked up as if to check a scoreboard in the sky and took a step, another, and soared into space – a surreal, cartoonish stick figure stuck against the blue Christian sky.

Chapter 23

On this bright day in Lent, in a remote America, far removed from world dangers and urban ethnic strife, in the cradle of Man's goodwill, in the presence of God, a kid who lived his life through others floated alone to his death.

Church bells tolled all week.

Pre-ministerial students prayed in the church. Preps knelt in the pews. Jocks, kneeling, holding each other's hands, teared up. Calvin professors, heads bowed, listened intently to the words of the Dean of Religious Studies. Norman Emory's father spoke, said; his son loved life and loved Calvin. Said only God understands.

His mother and sister, in veiled black, kneeled silently.

Hal Sparrow, the Player, wondered if he would ever find his voice.

Chapter 24

It was the following Monday after class when Hal returned to his room off campus. There was an envelope on the table past the front door entrance addressed to him, postmarked Lewisburg. Unusual, he thought, seldom receiving mail, and who from this town would send him a letter? Couldn't be a bill.

His name and address were written in the hand of Norman Emory, and that sent an array of shivers down his spine.

With creeping trepidation, he walked it to his room, kicked off his shoes, and lay down on his bed. With fumbling fingers, he opened the letter, took a deep breath, and read.

Dear Hal, my splendid Player.

I wrote this letter after returning to the dorm from our talk. It's the "why," I'm sure you are wondering. The only one I care about wondering. To you with love.

I beg you to keep this information confidential. I can trust no one else. My love for you will accompany me on the journey began Friday.

You were good to hear me out though it wasn't all out. And before I tell you what that means, let me tell you once more, and for the last time, what you have meant to me, even in the relative absence of contact we had in our last three years. There is no one outside of my family I've met who I admire more. It's your character, your rigid honesty, your sense of fairness, and your perseverance in overcoming obstacles that would have defeated most others.

My decision Friday to end my life was based upon one more situation I didn't share with you. I felt I had totally overburdened you with my parents' problems (which I learned on a call I finally had with them before coming out to the Quarry was even worse than I had imagined,) my loss of the job I so desired, and its probable effect on Carrie's being able to financially afford college at the University of Pittsburgh.

You have, I believe, taken a class with the new head of the English department, Dr. Edward Johnson, in his second year here. Last semester I took two classes with him. He seemed to take an extra interest in me, maybe because I was so motivated by his lectures. I would hang around after class with a score of questions for him. After one class, he asked me to write five pages on the difference in writing style between Dickens and Jane Austen. I brought it to class a week later, and he invited me to come over to his house and discuss it. And so our special teacher/student relationship began.

With his patient personal guidance of my learning of other art forms, I began feeling magically alive, saturated in a new world of light. Doctor Johnson, as you know, came to Calvin from his professor position at Hunter University in Manhattan. He's the most sophisticated man I have ever met. From that first class with him, 19th Century English Poets, I was enamored with his brilliance, with his wit. I began, at his invitation, visiting his house after dinner to work on learning, to figuratively sit at his feet, the master of knowledge. I wanted to know everything he knew. He was a bachelor, and that made our moments discussing great novels and novelists more personal, uncluttered with noise from others. It was ecstasy.

I had never been in the interior of any house like his. The living room was encircled by wall-attached bookshelves, a personal library of great breadth. He had a collection of 78RPM classical music albums with stereo speakers that made listening to an idyllic experience, a time when we set aside words and wafted through a wonderland of introspection. At least that's what I felt when these short-lived moments became an evening-ending routine, a wordless departure into an ethereal sanctuary of the mind. Is that poetic, Hal, my Player? He also kept in his small but intimate den a decanter of sherry wine, a sweet drink I had never tasted.

Why am I telling you all this, Hal? Because by the time you read it, I will be gone and with nothing more to give, to share with anyone else. I'll not be a failure, or a burden to my parents ever again.

Back to Doctor Johnson. Soon, maybe six months later, we were engaged in a relationship. Remember Hadrian and his disciple? That was us, except no one knew anything about it. Our secret. Of course, I never told my parents, who by this time may have had an idea I was queer. But I did share the story of my love with Carrie. She sounded happy.

About six months ago, right before the Christmas break, when I brought him a gift, an out-of-print book about the history of this region, he had exciting news. He was one of two finalists for a position at Columbia University in New York, an assistant head of the English Language department.

To finalize his candidacy, he was asked to write a twenty-thousand-word paper on the monarchial, intellectual, cultural, and economic influences on the development of the English language. It would be easy for him, A slam dunk in our basketball lexicon, but he wanted more information and assigned me the job of researching the library at Carnegie Mellon which I did in a day's visit there over the Christmas vacation.

When it came to writing the final paper, he asked me to write a few pages on what I found to be, in his view, a rare insight into the cultural impacts based on the writings of an obscure historian. I submitted three thousand words on this insight, not always providing identification of direct quotations of the author.

Two weeks later, he asked a number of questions about my work on this research, and I answered, of course, honestly but a bit hastily. It was a moment when I was in preparation for the first semester exams, and I was behind on my newspaper columns.

I fucked up.

He submitted a number of paragraphs I had written. A month ago came the word that he had plagiarized the writing of the author I had found. The Dean of the University's department told him it was a major consideration for him not getting the position.

He was crushed. More bad news occurred when he was told by our Calvin president that they had received belated and confirmed information that he had misrepresented details of his student performance on his application to Calvin. That was not all. He had written two checks to me over this period of time. How the school found out about these small checks, loans, he said, to help me through this last semester remains a mystery, but the president of the bank here in Lewisburg is a trustee of the university. This, said the attorney for the college, raised concerns. Was he concerting with a student, one Norman Emory? The attorney's advice was for him to seek job opportunities, and the college will never mention why he left. While it may still remain a secret, Doctor Johnson will not be back at Calvin next year.

Our relationship was destroyed. I can't tell how devastating our final meeting was; the words are too painful to repeat, even as they would be among my last. He has refused to see me since.

Hal, I hope you will forgive me.

I feel I have nothing to contribute to society. I am too fragile to rebound from my misery and failure. I will depart this world with great remorse, with few fond memories of life beyond repair. I think out, out brief candle.

Good night, Sweet Prince.

Norman Emory.

CPSIA information can be obtained
at www.ICGtesting.com
Printed in the USA
LVHW050800210223
739942LV00010BA/295